FALLING FOR HIM

OAK BROOK ACADEMY, BOOK 2

JILLIAN ADAMS

JILLIANADAMS.COM

ONE

Perched on the top corner of the bleachers, I watched as the football team ran onto the field. Their uniforms sparkled in the sunlight as they bounded across the rich green grass.

"Anything for the football team." I rolled my eyes, then made a note on the notebook that I balanced on one knee.

How much did the uniforms cost?

How much for the upkeep of the football field?

I underlined each question, then pulled out my phone to start on some research. A splashy headline wouldn't mean anything if I couldn't back it up with some solid evidence. Despite being rejected by Mr. Raynaud, who supervised the Oak Brook Academy school newspaper, I had no intention of backing off of my theory that the football players and the cheerleaders were grossly over-funded compared to the rest of the clubs and activities at the school.

I pushed my shoulder-length blonde hair back over my shoulders and focused on the group of boys on the field. I knew a few of them quite well. We'd been going to school together for two years. Others I'd barely met, due to my isolation from the in-crowd. I didn't mind being on the fringe. It allowed me to see the truth more clearly. Ever since I'd joined the school paper, I'd taken my introduction to journalism very seriously.

I made another note on my notepad, then heard a shout. I looked up in time to see a football flying straight toward the stands. There wasn't time to think about how it had been thrown in that direction or why, as it was headed straight for my face. Although logically I knew I should duck forward, there wasn't time for logic either. Instead, I lunged backward and toppled right off the bleachers.

As I fell, I caught sight of the wide-open blue sky above me.

My day hadn't started out like this. I'd coached myself as I'd made my way to the football field, promising that I'd find a break in my investigation. I'd been determined to insert myself into the world of the student athletes, no matter what it took.

I hadn't expected to fall off the bleachers.

I braced myself as I anticipated slamming into the hard ground.

Instead, I slammed into a hard chest and strong arms.

"Hang on, I've got you, Alana," a warm voice murmured in my ear as those strong arms tightened around me.

I tipped my head to the side to look into the eyes of the person who'd caught me. Rich chocolate eyes stared back at me, heated with concern.

"Are you okay?"

I recognized him right away. How could I not? He always seemed to be around. The darling of the football team and right in the middle of the in-crowd, Mick always found a way to be the center of attention.

"Fine, thanks." I stammered and then swallowed hard. "Maybe you could put me down now?"

"Oh, sure." He chuckled, his cheeks flushed. "Sorry, I just wanted to make sure that you weren't hurt." He eased me down to the ground.

Several other football players and a handful of cheerleaders encircled us with curious stares.

"Man, I didn't even know someone was in the bleachers!" One of the football players stepped forward. "I swear, I wasn't aiming at you."

"I'm sure you weren't." I did my best to remain calm as I faced down an entire crowd of the very people I intended to investigate. "I guess I put on my cloak of invisibility today." I cracked an awkward smile.

"Your what?" The football player, whom I recognized as a boy named Graham, blinked at me.

"Never mind." I rolled my eyes as I heard Mick chuckle beside me.

"You're not going to tell the principal, are you?" Graham took a step closer to me. "I didn't mean it, you have to believe me."

I squinted at him, uncertain whether to believe him. I'd been the target of bullies before. Not too often, but I found it hard to believe that he'd managed to throw the football directly at me by accident—almost as hard as it was to believe that Mick just happened to be walking behind the bleachers when I'd fallen. However, I knew that the more I alienated the team, the less likely it would be for me to find the proof I was looking for to include in my article.

"I guess I don't have to say anything to him. But how are you going to make it up to me?"

"Listen to this one!" Sherry, one of the cheerleaders I recalled from middle school, gave a sharp shriek. "She's got you now, Graham!"

"I mean, what do you want?" His stunned green eyes met mine. "If I get in trouble again, I'm going to get kicked off the team."

"Sure, the principal is going to kick his best quarterback off the football team over me?" I shook my head as I laughed. "That's not likely."

"You think I'm the best?" Graham flashed me a smile as he raised an eyebrow.

"That's not exactly what I said." I shifted from one foot to the other.

"Sounded like it." Mick cleared his throat from just behind me. "So how are you going to make it up to her, Graham?"

"How about dinner?" Graham smirked. "My treat. I'll take you anywhere you want."

"What?" Sherry snapped at him.

"Relax, babe, it's just a make-it-up-to-you-date." Graham shrugged as he looked at her.

"Sounds thrilling." I crossed my arms. "Not interested, sorry."

"Ouch." Mick punched Graham's shoulder. "Looks like that charm isn't going to win her over."

"Okay, so what? Do you want cash?" Graham frowned.

"I don't need your money." My heart pounded as I realized that this was my opportunity. This was my one chance to infiltrate the football team and find out the truth. I shifted my attention from Graham to Sherry. "I want a spot on the cheerleading squad."

"A what?" Sherry stared at me. "Girls train all year to be a part of this squad. You can't just buy your way in."

"Sure she can." Graham placed his hand on Sherry's shoulder. "Get her an outfit, babe."

"It's a uniform." She shot him an impatient look.

I stared at the two of them. Would it really work? Was this the break I'd hoped for?

"I've been taking gymnastics since I was two, Sherry, I'm sure I can handle it." I met her eyes. At seventeen, Sherry looked like a supermodel. From her curly red hair to her perfect legs, she drew the attention of everyone who looked in her direction.

I, on the other hand, was short. That was pretty much the extent of my description. Short. Too short for most sports. Certainly too short for the cheerleading squad. Although I'd been in gymnastics from a young age, my body was still thick and rounded in places that I guessed Sherry's had never been.

I didn't blame her for looking at me with distaste, but that was part of the problem—part of the story I was writing. High school sports were supposed to be for everyone, not just the elite or the pretty. But the athletic clubs at Oak Brook Academy were filled with picture-perfect specimens that all seemed to be best buddies. Anyone that didn't look like them, or worship them, didn't stand a chance of getting picked.

"Fine, whatever." Sherry rolled her eyes. "But just for the rest of the season. If you want to join next year, you'll have to try out like everyone else."

"Great." I stuck my hand out to Graham. "It's been great doing business with you."

"I'll bet." He glared at me as he shook my hand. "I'm going to pay for this, you know."

"Well, maybe next time you'll look before you throw." I smiled sweetly, then turned toward Sherry. "When do I start?"

"Let's get you a uniform." She sighed and gestured for me to follow her.

"Alana, wait." Mick grabbed my arm to stop me.

"What?" I glanced over my shoulder at him.

"I didn't know you were interested in cheerleading." He stared hard into my eyes.

"I'm sure there's plenty that you don't know about me." I flashed him a smile, pulled my arm free, then jogged after Sherry.

TWO

I'd been inside the locker room before—during gym class and while reporting on hidden health hazards at the school. My article had inspired a cleaning schedule change for the whole school. But I'd never been there as a member of a team.

As Sherry walked over to the supply closet, I watched her perfect curls bounce in front of me.

"I can't believe I'm doing this." She huffed as she tugged a box out of the closet. "You know, I doubt if we even have anything in your size."

"Probably not." I frowned and did my best not to take her comment personally. It didn't matter; I wasn't there for her approval. I was there because I wanted to find out some inside information. "I guess it's not in the budget to get another one, huh? You've probably already spent your max on uniforms this year."

"The max?" Sherry laughed and shook her head. "No, we don't have a max. If we want a new uniform, all we have to do is ask for it." She held up a uniform that was far too tiny to fit me. "Do you think you can squeeze into this one?"

"No." I narrowed my eyes. "Why not just order me one if it's so simple?"

"Because I don't want you to have a brand new one." She dropped the uniform, then picked up another. "In fact, I don't want you to have one at all, but I have no choice, do I?" She tossed the uniform at me. "Make it fit. You seem to be pretty good at getting what you want."

"It's not my fault he threw the ball at me." I caught the uniform and scowled at her. "I was just sitting there."

"Yeah, and you had no reason to be there. Don't think I don't know what you were doing up there. You and your judgmental little smirk." She stared at me. "I don't know what your game is, Alana, but I'm going to be watching you. Practice starts in five minutes. You'd better be out there in uniform or you're off the team." She snapped her fingers, then stalked out of the locker room.

I stared after her, stunned by her attitude. It didn't surprise me that she could be nasty. It surprised me that I didn't know how to react to it. I'd spent quite a few years trying to become immune to the way the popular girls looked at me, but apparently it hadn't worked.

My heart pounded as I wondered what I'd gotten myself into. I could easily just walk out of the locker room and forget everything that had happened. I could abandon the article that nobody wanted me to write anyway. In two years, Oak Brook Academy would be nothing but a memory. But what about the next girl that started out as a freshman at the Academy? What if she didn't fit the mold of what the athletes were supposed to look like?

I took a deep breath, then looked at the uniform again. It would take some serious wedging, but I would have to find a way to make it work. As I changed into it, I did my best not to criticize my body. I knew it wasn't smooth or slim, but I also knew that it served me well and not every girl was meant to look identical to the next.

A look in the mirror, however, revealed that the uniform was far from flattering. The stitches stretched so far it looked like they might burst. Yes, Sherry had done this on purpose. She'd put me in an impossible position. Either I had to go out there and embarrass myself or I had to give up on the whole idea. But what Sherry didn't know about me was that I didn't give up easily.

I smoothed my hair back into a ponytail, took a very shallow breath to prevent stitch-popping, then marched out onto the field.

As I walked past the cluster of football players, my cheeks burned. I could feel them looking at me. Of course they were. I'd just threatened to get their best player kicked off the team. Why wouldn't they be looking at me?

"One foot in front of the other, Alana." I stared straight ahead as I continued to walk toward the gathering of cheer-leaders.

"Oh my!" Sherry burst out laughing as she looked at me. "You must be so uncomfortable. I'm so sorry, hon, but that was the biggest uniform I could find. I guess we just don't have your size."

"It's fine." I forced a smile on my lips. "I'm ready to practice."

"I'll bet you are." Sherry glared at me, then turned to the other girls. "I'd like you to meet our newest member. This is Alana and we're stuck with her until the end of the season." She held up one hand. "Don't ask me why, I don't want to talk about it. Just pretend she isn't here and we'll all get through this."

The other girls stared at me with curled lips and sharp stares. I certainly wasn't going to be welcomed with open arms. Maybe if I threatened to turn Graham in after all, she'd be more friendly, but I didn't want to push it. Sherry was doing something she didn't want to do for the sake of her boyfriend, but she might not play along if I made things too hard on her.

As the girls began to practice their routine, I felt a subtle draw. It had been awhile since I'd done any leaps or tumbles and the sensation of flying through the air was something that I missed. I studied their movements, curious about whether I could pull them off. As I memorized them, I began to feel the urge to participate. What was the point of my being on the squad if I couldn't get inside the heads of the cheerleaders?

"I think I could keep up." I walked over to Sherry. "How about I join in?"

"No way." Sherry glared at me. "You've got the uniform, that's it."

"What could you even do?" another girl sneered. "We are real athletes, you know. We don't just shake our pom-poms."

"I know." I frowned, remembering my excitement as a freshman. I'd heard about the cheerleading squad and how impressive it was. I'd looked forward to showing off my experience in gymnastics at the try-outs. But I hadn't even been allowed to try out. There'd been a pre-screening process that included the captain laughing at me. My cheeks burned at the memory. Maybe it had been foolish of me to be there.

As the other girls went back to their routine, my stomach twisted. No, I didn't look like them, but that didn't mean I couldn't move like them.

Determined to prove that point, I launched into a cartwheel followed by a double back flip. As my feet struck the ground in a perfect landing, I smiled in the same moment that a terrible sound greeted my ears.

"Oh my." Sherry covered her mouth as she laughed. "Talk about letting it rip!"

Horrified, I looked down at my uniform to find that it was

nothing but a flapping piece of material. The stretched stitches had given up on trying to hold together and the seams of the uniform had burst. The light breeze that carried through the field was enough to reveal just about every part of me.

"How embarrassing!" another girl giggled. "Get it? Em-bare—"

"We got it, alright, Shannon." Sherry burst out laughing.

I clutched at the material in an attempt to cover myself, but it was in such tatters that it wasn't much help.

"Alright, guys, let's get her to the locker room." A girl stepped forward and I recognized her as a friend of a friend.

"Hallie, back off." Sherry pointed her finger at her. "She needs to experience this. She thinks she can just walk on this field and be one of us and she's wrong. She needs to be taught a lesson." Sherry turned back to look at me. "Go on, see how far you can make it to the locker room without giving the whole football team a show. Or maybe that's why you wanted to be part of the squad in the first place? To get their attention? Really." She sucked her teeth, then shook her head. "Shameful."

"Enough, Sherry. Leave her alone," Hallie said in a quiet voice.

THREE

Just don't cry; whatever you do, don't cry. I repeated the words in my head as I endured Sherry's barrage of insults. The humiliation I felt was beyond comprehension, but I knew that if I let a single tear fall, I would never live it down. Instead, I had to make that long walk to the locker room as if it didn't bother me at all. But how could I do that? I'd never even worn a bikini, let alone paraded across a field in my underpants. And yes, the football team had noticed—and yes, they were watching.

I bit into my bottom lip in an attempt to stop the urge to cry. Maybe if I hadn't started all this, I wouldn't be in this position.

"Here, I'll walk with you." Hallie stepped up behind me. "They won't be able to see anything."

"Hallie, I swear if you don't get back in line right now, you're off the squad." Sherry pointed to the line of cheerleaders that watched my every move. "It's your choice."

"Sherry, you're being ridiculous." Hallie rolled her eyes but took a step back toward her.

"It's okay." I met her eyes. My voice trembled a little, but I tried to ignore it. "It's no big deal." I took a deep breath and turned toward the locker room. Maybe I was mortified, but I didn't have to let them know that. I could hide it, I could walk with pride. I took a few steps and the back of the uniform blew up into the air. I shivered, both from the breeze and from the exposure.

"Hey, Alana!" one of the football players shouted at me.

I closed my eyes. Were they really going to harass me for the entire walk back to the locker room? Of course they were.

Just don't cry, Alana. I clenched my teeth together as hard as I could.

"Alana, wait." I heard the voice again and this time, I recognized it. Mick jogged up beside me.

I did my best not to look at him.

He pulled off his jersey and held it out to me. "Here, put this on."

I stared at him for a moment. Was it some kind of trick?

His warm brown eyes met mine and he smiled some. "In case you're cold, you know. It's a little windy out here."

"Thanks." I took the jersey from him cautiously. I guessed that he must be up to something. As I started to put it on, my uniform rose into the air.

He caught the skirt of it and tugged it back down. I felt the warmth of his fingers as they glided along my thigh in the process. "Let me help you." He took the jersey back and dropped it over the top of my head.

I felt engulfed by the huge shirt and by Mick's scent, which clung to it. It was a mixture of deodorant, sweat, and a hint of cologne. The shirt came down almost to my knees and covered up what the ripped uniform had exposed.

As I slid my arms into it, I heard the laughter of the cheerleaders and a few shouts from the football players, but all I could see was Mick's eyes, still gazing into mine.

"Don't let them get to you, Alana."

"I won't." I managed a small smile, then turned and walked

toward the locker room. As strange as it was to be given Mick's shirt, I was grateful for it. He didn't have to step out of the crowd and help me. He could have teased me like the cheerleaders or harassed me like the football players. Instead, he'd made a chivalrous move, and although I wasn't sure what his motive was, it made an impression.

As soon as I was alone in the locker room, I burst into tears. Hot and fast, they slid down my cheeks as I sat down on one of the benches between the lockers. Sometimes I felt so confident, so certain of myself, convinced I could do anything. And other times, I wished I didn't even exist. This was one of those moments as I replayed the incident in my mind over and over. I should have just stood there. Or better yet, I never should have been on the bleachers. The other girls were right: I didn't belong anywhere near the athletic field

I remembered the blue sky above me as I fell and the shock of slamming into Mick's chest and arms. He'd rescued me twice that afternoon. I knew that he was good friends with my friend Maby. I guessed that maybe that was why he had stepped out to help me.

I wiped my cheeks before any tears could get on his shirt. I imagined him standing out there in nothing but a t-shirt and his pads. Did he regret helping me? Were the other boys giving him a hard time? I pushed the thoughts of him from my mind and pulled his jersey off. How strange the day had turned out to be. Despite the ripped uniform and the humiliation I'd experienced, I was still on the squad. I was still close to getting to the truth. I wanted that more than anything. I wouldn't give up, even if it meant a million more embarrassing moments.

As I pulled my clothes back on, I stared down at the tattered uniform on the bench. Maybe it was the largest one they had. Maybe Sherry would use that as her excuse to kick me off the team. I gathered it up, tucked it into my backpack, then picked up Mick's jersey

I started toward the door when the memory of the scent that had surrounded me resurfaced in my mind. I wasn't ready to forget it. I brought the jersey to my face and took another sniff and for just a moment, I recalled the warmth in those big brown eyes.

"Oh no, none of that, Alana." I folded up the jersey, tucked it under my arm, and stepped out of the locker room.

As I did, I bumped right into Hallie.

"Hey, are you okay?" She stared at me, her lips curved into a frown.

"I'm fine, thanks." I hoped that she didn't notice my puffy eyes or red cheeks.

"I'm sorry about earlier. Sherry can be such a pain. I wanted to help." She sighed.

"It's alright. I know you can't risk being kicked off the team. You're friends with Maby, right?"

"Yes, I am. We don't hang out as much as we used to, but I've seen you with her."

"Thanks for trying to help." I shrugged. "I knew this wouldn't be easy, but I didn't expect that to happen."

"She probably gave you a really old uniform." She glanced over her shoulder, then spoke in a soft voice. "Look, she's not going to stop giving you a hard time, but I wanted you to know that you looked amazing out there. Those flips were perfect."

"Thanks." A bit of warmth brewed in my chest.

"Stick it out if you can." She whispered again. "Sherry will never admit this, but our team could really use someone like you. The other girls just aren't as skilled."

"I'll try." I flashed her a brief smile, then shied back as Sherry and the rest of the squad headed down the hall. "You'd better go before they catch you talking to me."

"Right." Hallie rolled her eyes, then stepped past me into the locker room.

I walked off in the other direction. All I wanted to do was get back to my dorm room and as far away from Sherry and the rest of the cheerleaders as I could. If I had been an outsider before, I was now untouchable. I doubted I would ever be able to get the information I needed.

As I headed for the girls' dormitory, I tried to forget the afternoon. My uniform had never ripped. I never flashed the whole football team. None of it ever happened.

"Alana!" His voice broke through my brainwashing.

I glanced over my shoulder as Mick jogged toward me. Mick, with his thick chest and his strong arms. Mick, with that sweet and salty smell that I just couldn't forget.

FOUR

As my mind swam, I tried not to think about the strange feeling that he'd stirred in me. It didn't matter. He'd helped me because he was friends with Maby, not because he had any interest in my well-being. But why was he after me now?

I turned around to face him, prepared to be the brunt of some kind of practical joke. He probably needed to prove himself to his buddies. He didn't actually want to do anything to help me.

"What is it?" I crossed my arms and only then realized that I still had his jersey tucked under one.

"My jersey." He frowned as he stopped in front of me. "I kind of need it back."

"Oh right, I meant to give it back to you." I held it out to him. "I got distracted."

"I just need it because I have to have it for the game tomorrow." He locked his eyes to mine. "I saw your moves out there on the field. They were pretty great."

"My moves?" I shook my head. "All I remember is ripped stitches."

JILLIAN ADAMS

"Don't worry about that." He chuckled. "They'll forget about it in no time."

"Really?"

"No." He sighed, then shrugged. "But all you can do is get through it."

"Thanks for the jersey." I started to turn back toward the door of the dormitory.

"Wait." He stepped up beside me. "You know, tomorrow night after the game there's a party."

"A party?" I looked over at him.

"Yes. All the players and the cheerleaders will be there. I thought maybe you would like to come with me." He met my eyes. "As my date."

"Your date?" I laughed. "Is this the joke?" I looked around behind him. "Where are your friends hiding? Are they all going to pop out and laugh at me? Or is someone taking video to post online?" I narrowed my eyes. "Just how stupid do you think I am?"

"I don't think you're stupid at all." He rubbed his hand along the back of his neck. "But now I think you might be a little paranoid."

"I'm not paranoid. Just realistic." I pursed my lips. "I don't know what this is all about, but I don't like it."

"Alright, fair enough. If you don't like me, you can just say that." He took a step back. "I'm not trying to force you into anything."

"Are you serious?" I stared, uncertain what to expect from him. I had one idea in my head of who Mick was, but he certainly was acting different.

"Yes, I'm serious." He shrugged. "But if you don't want to go, that's fine too."

My mind flooded with possibilities. Mick could be my way into the crowd of athletes and cheerleaders. A way that I never

20

expected to have. Sure, he couldn't possibly like me, but that didn't mean I couldn't play along with his ploy long enough to find out what was going on behind closed doors. Sherry certainly wasn't going to invite me to the party.

"Alright." I nodded as I studied him. "Sure, I'll go with you."

"Great." He smiled. "You can ride with me after the game. The players and the cheerleaders get special permission to go off school grounds after the games. Sherry's mother has a house in the area that we use for the parties."

"I see." My stomach churned at the idea of being caught up in some wild party, but if it meant I'd get information for my story, I was willing to tolerate it. Of course it didn't hurt that Mick's eyes were just so beautiful. I forced myself to look away. "Okay, see you then." I turned to the door and this time Mick didn't stop me.

When I glanced back over my shoulder as I stepped through the door, I found that he was still there—watching me. Again I felt a ripple of fear. What did he have in mind for me? Was it some kind of long prank that would end up being more embarrassing than being practically naked on the football field?

When I reached my dorm, my roommate Cyndi threw open the door.

"Tell me right this second what you were doing out there with Mick!" She grinned as she pulled me inside.

"Were you spying on me?" I frowned as I tossed my bag on the sofa.

"A little. I heard some rumors about what happened on the football field and I wanted to make sure that you were okay."

"Thanks." I pulled the cheerleading uniform out of my bag. "This is all that's left." I frowned. "It was pretty bad."

"Maybe, but that still doesn't explain what happened with Mick! I also don't understand why you're even on the cheerleading squad. Did you even try out?" She looked me over. "You don't seem like the cheerleading type."

"You're right, I'm not." I carried the uniform over to the sewing machine set up on the kitchen table in the small kitchenette we shared. "But things happened, and for now, I am." I glanced at her.

I liked Cyndi, but I didn't know if I could trust her with the truth. If word got out about why I was really on the squad, I'd be kicked off right away.

"Things happened with Mick?" She sat down across from me at the table.

I dug through my materials bag for a color similar to the uniform. "Yes, I guess they did. He asked me to go to a party with him after the game tomorrow."

"Wait, what?" She rocked back in her chair. "You're going on a date with Mick? He must really like you."

"Oh please, I know why he asked me out." I adjusted the needle on the sewing machine and studied the rip in the material of the uniform.

"You do?" Cyndi raised an eyebrow. "It's not because he likes you?"

"No way. He's Mick." I looked up at her and shook my head. "A boy like him? He could have any girl at this school. Trust me, he's not about to pick a girl like me."

"Don't be ridiculous. You're gorgeous. I saw you turning that one guy's head. Oh, what's his name? He's always hanging out with Maby and her crew." She frowned. "I don't know, but the point is, you get plenty of interest, you just don't return it."

"The thing is, I don't want just interest." I lined up the material with the uniform and pressed down on the pedal of the sewing machine. "It seems like boys our age are only looking for a date to a party or someone to make out with behind the bleachers. I don't know—I guess I want more than that. I figure I'll have to wait until I graduate to get that."

"Especially if you don't give any guy a chance." Cyndi sighed. "Have you ever thought there might be some boys that feel the same way you do?"

"Maybe. I guess it's possible. But, even if there are, Mick certainly isn't one of them. You have to at least admit that." I turned the material and continued to sew.

"Yeah, you're probably right about that. He's not exactly the serious type." Cyndi looked at the uniform I held up. "Wow, that looks great. Did you really dance around naked on the field?"

"Is that what people are saying?" I sighed.

"Oh, that's the mildest thing people are saying." She laughed.

"Great." I rolled my eyes. "I guess tomorrow's game should be fun."

"I can't believe you're really going to be out there cheering." Cyndi frowned. "I guess I'll have to find someone else to hang out with."

"What do you mean?" I met her eyes. Was she too embarrassed to be my friend?

"I mean that you're part of that crowd now, Alana. They'll suck you in real fast and the rest of us—the normal people—we'll stop existing to you."

"That's not true. They're not my friends and they're never going to be. You are." I smiled at her as I remembered how warmly she'd greeted me when I arrived at the dorm earlier that year. Sure, she was shy and she tended to hide behind her books, but she'd made sure that I'd felt welcome and she'd been a great friend ever since.

FIVE

I woke up Saturday morning with a knot in my stomach. For a few seconds I held my breath and hoped that everything that had happened the day before was just a dream. As the seconds ticked by, however, and no giant dinosaur traipsed through my room, I began to face the fact that this was my new reality.

I sat up in bed and wiped at my eyes. If I was going to survive the day and night, I knew I would need reinforcements. After a quick breakfast, I left Cyndi a note, then headed over to Maby's dorm. Our friendship picked up out of the blue not long ago, and although I didn't expect it to lead anywhere, it felt as if she'd taken me under her wing in some way. Of course, after what had happened the day before, she might want nothing to do with me.

I knocked on her door, then waited for her to answer.

"Oh, would you look at you." Maby leaned against the door jam and smiled. "You're just causing a stir, aren't you?"

"I didn't dance on the field naked."

"No, I didn't think you did." She laughed, then pulled me inside her dorm room. "Tell me all about it." She led me into her bedroom. "Just keep it down, Sophie's still sleeping."

"Sure." I glanced in the direction of her roommate's bedroom. Sophie was new, and although she seemed nice enough, I didn't feel that she liked me all that much. "So, I joined the cheerleading squad."

"Ha—no, you didn't." She stared at me as she sat down in the swivel chair at her desk. "Try telling me the truth."

I squirmed under her steady stare. Maby had such confidence that at times she came across as quite intimidating.

"That's what happened." I cleared my throat.

"No, it's not. No one just joins the cheerleading squad. The captain handpicks the girls that make the squad at the beginning of the year. No exceptions. So how exactly did you manage to get a spot?" She continued to stare at me.

I considered my options. I could keep lying to Maby and she'd see right through it, which might make her suspicious of my motives, or I could tell her part of the truth.

"Okay, Graham might have thrown a football at my head and in exchange for not turning him in to the principal, Sherry offered me a spot on the squad." I raised an eyebrow. "I certainly turned that down."

"Huh." She continued to watch me. "Do you know what you're doing, Alana?"

"Sure." I sat down on the edge of her bed.

"No, I mean, do you really know what you're doing?" She walked over and sat down beside me. "Sherry doesn't play games. She seeks and destroys."

"I'm not scared of her." I forced the words past the lump in my throat.

"Well, it'll help that you have Mick on your side." She began to run her fingers through my hair. "We need to do something about this flat mop." She directed me to her vanity. "Sit down, I'll see what I can do."

"I'm not sure that Mick's on my side." I sat down in front of her vanity.

"He told me he asked you to the party tonight and you said yes." She smiled. "You two would make such a cute couple."

"We're not a couple." I felt my muscles tense, despite how relaxing it was for her to play with my hair.

"Not yet, but you're going to go with him, right?" Maby adjusted the part in my hair, then looked at my reflection in the mirror.

"Yes, of course." I smiled as I turned to look at her. "I mean, why wouldn't I?"

"No reason. I just know you can be a little picky." Maby shrugged.

"Me? You think I'm picky?" I laughed. "Why?"

"Why? You haven't been on a date since we've started hanging out. So I just assumed."

"I haven't been on a date because no one has asked me." I stood up from the chair. "Mick asked, so I'm going."

"Good. Mick's a real good guy." Maby walked over to her closet and opened it up. "Do you need anything for the party? Shoes? Scarf?"

"No, I think I'll be fine." I watched as she sorted through her things.

Although I really liked Maby, I wasn't sure yet if I could trust her. She said that Mick was a good catch, but how did she know that? Because he was on the football team? Because he hung out with her?

Whether or not he was a good guy, he was Alana's way in and she was going to milk it for all that it was worth.

"You know these parties." Maby turned around to face me with a long feather boa of multi-colored feathers grasped in her hands. "They can get a little wild. Are you sure you're ready for this?" She met my eyes as she draped the boa around my neck.

"I'm sure I can handle it. Aren't you going to be there?"

"Oh no, strictly football players and cheerleaders. I went to a few as Mick's date." She smiled. "Just as friends, of course."

"If he's such a good guy, why have you only just been friends?" I looked at her and tugged the boa free from my neck.

"He's just not my type." She shrugged. "We make better friends than lovers. That is how it is with most guys I meet. Anyway, that doesn't mean he wouldn't be perfect for you. Did you pick out a dress?"

"I have a few. Definitely something with good stitching." I grinned.

"I love that about you, Alana." Maby shook her head. "You're always quick to laugh at yourself."

"How can I not? It was a disaster." I groaned and stood up from the vanity. "I think I'm going to need more than a new hairstyle to live that down."

"You certainly have their attention right now." Maby walked me through the dorm to the door. "But that makes it the perfect time to use that attention. Whatever you do right now is going to have a powerful impact. So don't waste it." She grabbed her purse. "Let's go get you a few things for tonight. When I'm done with you, you're going to be getting attention for all the right reasons."

"I'm not sure I want any more attention." I shuddered at the memory of the sound of the rip.

"Trust me, with that crowd, you do. We just have to steer it in the right direction." She locked the door behind her, then led me out of the girls' dormitory. "Attention good or bad is always good, you just have to know how to use it."

"If you say so." I sighed as I trailed behind her. The day before, I hadn't even existed to these people; now I was their enemy. I recalled Maby's warning about what I was getting myself into. Was I really prepared for it? My stomach twisted as

I thought of the way Sherry had glared at me. There was no question in my mind that she was ready to seek and destroy, which meant I had to do my best not to be an easy target.

I only have to last long enough to get the truth, I reminded myself. Then I could fade back into the background again and everything would settle down. Now that I was this close, there was no chance that I'd back down.

SIX

After our shopping trip, I put on my repaired uniform and headed out to the football field. I knew I wouldn't be allowed to participate much, but I still had to show up. As far as any of the other cheerleaders knew, I was on the squad because I wanted to be.

As I stepped onto the field I noticed the football players were already there. My heart fluttered at the sight of the uniforms. Which one was Mick? I forced myself to look away.

No distractions, Alana.

I took a deep breath and continued toward the gathering of cheerleaders.

"Oh, you're here." Sherry glared at me. "And what did you do to that uniform?"

"It looks great." Hallie smiled.

"It's not an official uniform." Sherry crossed her arms. "Do you think the rules don't apply to you, Alana?"

"I didn't have anything else to wear and I wanted to be here to support the squad." I looked straight into Sherry's eyes. "I thought this would do until I get my bigger uniform, which I'm sure you ordered."

"Well, it won't."

"If you want me to sit out, I will, but I couldn't let the squad take the field without my support. I'm sure you'll all do great today." I smiled at each of the cheerleaders in turn, although most refused to look at me.

"Actually, Nancy is out sick, remember?" Hallie turned to Sherry. "Without her, we won't have enough girls for the routine."

"We'll do a different one." Sherry shrugged.

"You know all of our routines need at least eight girls and we only have seven." Hallie glanced at me. "No, we actually have eight. So why don't we use her? I can teach her. I'm sure with her skills she'll pick it up really fast."

"Ugh." Sherry balled her hands into fists. "Fine. But don't get used to this, Alana. As soon as Nancy is back, you're on the bench."

"I understand." I held back a smile. I didn't expect to get to participate, but now that I could, I was excited.

"Hurry!" Hallie grabbed my hand and led me over to an open area beside the bleachers. "This is a big night, so we need to make sure we get this right. If you show the rest of the squad how talented you are, Sherry won't be able to get away with benching you."

"Thanks, Hallie." I met her eyes as I began to stretch my legs. "Why are you helping me?"

"I'm on the cheerleading squad because it looks good for college and I love the sport. I'm hoping to continue in college. Sherry's my captain—I have to listen to her—but I don't have to like her." She frowned. "I don't know what happened between the two of you that got you on the team and made her hate you and I don't need to know. You're good for this squad. And you seem like a nice person." She smiled. "I'm always looking for a good friend."

"Me too." I smiled back at her, then followed her through the routine. As my body launched through the air, I felt the air brush against my skin and the freedom of momentary weightlessness.

In that instant, I forgot about my plans and savored the sensation.

As my feet struck the ground again, I heard loud clapping from a few feet away.

I spun around with a smile, expecting it to be Hallie. Instead it was Mick in full uniform. His eyes shined as he stared at me.

"Wow, I've never seen anyone move like that, Alana. That was amazing."

"Thanks." My heart raced and not just because of the exertion. The thought of him watching me go through the routine made me nervous and thrilled at the same time.

"You did that yourself?" He pointed to the extra material stitched into my uniform.

"Yes, it's just temporary." I smoothed down the skirt.

"It looks good. Multi-talented, huh?" He shook his head as he smiled at me. "I have to say, I'm impressed."

"Get out of here, Mick!" Hallie waved her hands at him. "Shoo! We have to practice!"

"Alright, I'm going." He stared at me a moment longer. "I'll pick you up at the dorm. For the party?"

"Right." I nodded to him as I tried to ignore the heat in my cheeks. "Good luck with the game."

"Thanks." He winked at me, then jogged off across the field.

"Wow, Mick, huh?" Hallie grinned. "You're going to have your hands full with that one."

"We're just friends. Let's practice." I began to run through the routine again.

"You've got it!" Hallie clapped as she nodded. "This is going to be great. Let's go before Sherry can think of a way to stop this from happening."

"I'm ready." I wished I felt as confident as I sounded. I knew I could do the routine, but after the uniform splitting experience the day before, I was nervous about running out onto the field in front of the entire school.

Luckily, I didn't have too long to be nervous, as minutes later we were on the field doing our first routine.

As I went through the motions of the routine, I felt a sense of belonging—not with the other cheerleaders, but in the sport. I recalled how disappointed I'd been when I hadn't been allowed to even try out for the squad. I wanted to make sure that no one else ever had to feel that way.

As the football game progressed, I found myself rooting for the team—mainly for Mick. As I watched him run across the field, I admired his strength and speed.

"Mm-hmm, number twenty-one definitely has skills." Hallie nudged my shoulder.

"I'm just watching the game."

"Sure. Part of the game." She grinned.

"Stop!" I laughed right as Sherry walked up to me.

"Don't get comfortable. Remember?" She glared at me. "You can show off as much as you want, but it's not going to change anything. Nancy will be back for the next game."

"I hope she is." I smiled at Sherry. "Thanks for the opportunity."

"Whatever." She rolled her eyes and walked away.

"How do you keep your cool with her?" Hallie shook her head. "I would lose it."

"I'm just happy to be part of all this." I jumped up and cheered as loud as I could when Mick scored the winning touchdown.

While the fans and the other players flooded the field, Mick ran in the other direction, straight toward me. I didn't realize his intentions until he scooped me up into his arms and spun me around.

"My good luck charm!" He grinned as his arms tightened around me.

I looked at him as I tried to catch my breath. I wanted to be annoyed that he would pick me up. I wanted to be irritated at his behavior. Instead, I was dizzy with happiness.

"You were fantastic!" I wrapped my arms around his neck for a quick hug. As I leaned in, his cheek brushed against mine and I felt the silk of his lips lightly brush against my ear. Electricity bolted through me in a way that I'd never experienced before.

I had to catch my breath again as I squirmed out of his arms.

He met my eyes, then opened his mouth to speak, but before he could Graham caught him by the arm and tugged him away to celebrate with the team.

"Just friends." Hallie smirked as she stepped up beside me. "Sure."

I watched as Mick's teammates rallied around him. When I'd started out this investigation, I hadn't thought twice about any of the players or the cheerleaders.

Now, with Hallie by my side and my heart still pounding with the memory of Mick's arms around me, I wondered who I might end up hurting when the truth came out.

SEVEN

That thought stuck in my mind as I walked back to the dorm. I tried to shake it loose from my head as I showered and then dressed. Hallie was sweet and I appreciated the possibility of having a new friend. Mick seemed to be the good guy that Maby described. But I still had a job to do and I took it very seriously.

I finished combing my hair, took a final glance in the mirror, then left my dorm room. The idea of going to the party caused butterflies in my stomach. Would I be accepted? Would Sherry insist that I leave? I had no idea what to expect.

I stepped through the door of the dormitory and found Mick just outside. There it was again—that spark. I did my best to ignore it as I walked over to him.

"You look beautiful." He smiled as he offered me his arm.

"Thanks." I brushed my hair back over my shoulders, then looped my arm around his.

It felt strange to walk beside him as if we were on a real date. I braced myself for what might come next. Were his buddies waiting around the corner to douse me with some foul liquid? Was I being recorded in case I'd made the foolish mistake of believing the date was real? Mick couldn't really be serious about me, could he?

"Are you okay?" He glanced over at me.

"Sure, I'm fine." I forced a smile.

"It's just that you're so quiet." He leaned closer to me. "You're not nervous, are you? About the party?"

"Maybe a little."

"I won't let them do anything to you." He frowned. "I'm sorry. I should have stopped them sooner yesterday."

"There's nothing to apologize for. Just a little playing around, right? I'm sure that it happens all the time." I bit into my bottom lip, then continued. "Especially on those bus trips you guys take. Is it true that you stayed in a penthouse last time?"

"Sure." He scrunched up his nose. "But it still smelled like a locker room."

"I'll bet." I grinned. "I guess you guys got room service too, huh? The school really spoiled you?"

"I don't really remember that much, to be honest." He glanced away from me, then coughed.

"You don't remember much about staying in a penthouse at one of the most expensive hotels in the state?" I laughed and tightened my arm around his.

"Like I said, I don't remember." His tone hardened as he looked at me. Then he smiled. "I heard you cheering when I made that touchdown."

"You did not." I let him change the subject, but I made note of his reaction. "Everyone was cheering."

"They were. But I heard you." He leaned his head close to mine. "Careful, Alana, or I might think you really like me." He pulled open the door of a taxi that waited just outside the school grounds.

"What's not to like?" I gave him a playful pat on the cheek as I stepped past him and slid into the taxi.

He settled in beside me and pulled the door closed.

This was it. I was really on a date with Mick.

He wrapped his hand around mine. "I saw your moves during the cheers. Very impressive."

"Thanks. It wasn't the winning touchdown, but I had a good time." I winked.

"Yes, today was a good day." He met my eyes. "But I think tonight is going to be even better."

I smiled, then looked out through the window of the taxi. Yes, there were sparks, but that didn't mean that anything was going to happen between us. To me, it was all business and I was sure that whatever his intentions were, they weren't good.

When we arrived at the party, the house was already full of people. Music blasted from all directions. Despite the massive size of the house, people were crowded into the hallways, the kitchen, the living room, and even up the stairs.

"I thought you said it would just be the players and the cheerleaders?" I looked over the crowd.

"Well, since we won, people went a little crazy with the invites." He grinned. "It's going to be an epic celebration."

"Looks like it."

"I'll get you a drink." He slid his arm free of mine.

"I don't drink."

"Don't worry, I was talking about a soda." He flashed me a grin, then disappeared into the crowd.

Once I was alone, the nervousness returned. It seemed like he had me in the perfect position for a prank. I took a deep breath and waited for it to happen.

When someone clapped me on the shoulder, I jumped.

"Wow, a little jumpy, huh?" Hallie laughed. "I'm glad you made it."

"I think you might be the only one." I looked around at the annoyed stares pointed in my direction.

"Me and Mick." She whispered in my ear. "His inviting you to the party hasn't made things any easier. The other girls are so jealous."

"Jealous?" I shook my head. "That's silly."

"It's true. Quite a few of them have been after Mick, including Sherry." She raised an eyebrow.

"But isn't Graham Sherry's boyfriend?"

"He is, but that's only because Mick turned her down. Oh look, here comes Graham now." I tipped my head toward the front door as he stepped inside.

I felt his gaze settle on mine. He held it for longer than he needed to, then turned his attention to the rest of the crowd.

"I can't hang around too long." Hallie flopped her long hair over one shoulder. "This isn't really my kind of thing. But I wanted to check on you."

"Thanks." I turned to face her. "I mean that."

"Good." She smiled as she met my eyes. "Just hang in there. I think you're going to do just fine."

"I'm going to try." I laughed.

Hallie walked away as Mick returned with a bottle of soda for me.

"Thanks."

"I wasn't sure if you liked diet. I took a chance."

"You guessed right." I cracked open the full-sugar bottle of soda and smiled. Someone turned the music up even louder. My head started to ache from the noise and the crowd but I ignored it.

Mick grabbed my hand and led me through the crowd out the back door. The party spilled out there as well surrounded a pool. The evening air was far too chilly for a swim, but a few people sat along the edge and dangled their feet in.

"It's quieter out here." He perched on an empty lounge chair and patted the spot beside him.

I sat down, aware of just how close he was. "I thought you'd prefer the party atmosphere."

"Well, that's why I brought you out here—because I think we should get to know each other better. For example, I do not prefer the party atmosphere. What about you?"

"Not really, no." I kicked my high heels off and tucked them under the chair. "So, what do you like to do with your time? Do you have any hobbies outside of football?"

"Football doesn't leave me a lot of time for other things. But I do enjoy drawing." He shrugged. "Not much of a hobby, though. And you? When you're not flying through the air, what do you like to do?"

"I read a lot." I stood up from the chair and walked toward the pool. "How do you think the water is?"

"Let's find out."

"What?" I started to turn to look at him, but as I did, someone slammed into me and I went crashing over the edge of the pool.

EIGHT

As I plunged into the cold water, I held my breath. My heart pounded and my mind spun. I had to get to the surface and fast.

As I swam upward, I heard cheers and laughter above the surface. Then several more splashes.

I broke through the water and looked straight into Mick's wide eyes as he paddled alongside me..

"So, how is it?"

"Are you kidding me?" I splashed water in his face. "Why would you do that to me?"

"Relax, it's a tradition." He grinned as he glanced over at several other people in the pool.

I noticed it was mainly couples—football players, cheerleaders, and maybe a handful of other people.

"Unbelievable." Fury pumped through my veins as I swam toward the edge of the pool.

"Alana, don't go, it'll get warmer the longer you're in here." He swam after me and caught me just as I started to climb out. "Stay, it's fun."

"This is not fun." I pushed his hand free of my arm and glared at him. "Go enjoy yourself."

"Are you telling me you didn't know about this?" He stared into my eyes. "All of the cheerleaders know."

"Not me." I shoved his hand away again and then finished climbing out of the pool. "It's a ridiculous thing to do."

"Alana, I'm sorry." He pulled himself out of the pool and followed after me. "I thought that's why you walked over to the edge of the pool. I thought you wanted me to."

"You thought wrong." I locked my eyes to his. "Don't follow me, I'm leaving."

"Alana, give me a chance here." He trailed after me despite my warning.

"I have nothing to say to you." I actually had a lot to say, but I decided against it. What was the point of wasting my energy on someone like him? He was obviously just like the rest of his football pals. "I'm sure you can find another cheerleader to push into the water."

"Stop." He caught my hand by the wrist as I reached the front door.

"No, you stop." I twisted my hand free. "I don't know what you're used to, Mick, but I'm not going to be pushed around just because you scored the winning touchdown. I don't care how hot you think you are and I don't care how hot anyone else thinks you are. Just leave me alone." I pushed my way through the door and continued down the sidewalk out into the street.

"How are you going to get home?" he called out to me from the door.

"Not your problem!" I shouted back and began to walk down the street. The truth was, I had no idea how I was going to get home. In fact, I didn't even know where we were.

Once we'd gotten in the taxi, I didn't think to ask where we were going. I didn't pay attention to what direction we were headed in. And since my phone was in my purse when Mick pushed me in the water, I doubted it would be in working condition.

I squeezed a bit of water from the skirt of my dress and realized that I only had one option. Public transportation—barefoot in a soaking wet dress. I'd never even taken a bus, let alone tried to navigate the subway or hail a taxi for myself.

I walked for about fifteen minutes before a car pulled up beside me, then slowed to a crawl to match my pace.

"Alana, right?" Graham looked out the window at me.

"Yes." I continued to walk.

"This is crazy. Get in the car."

"No thanks, I'll be fine." I shot a brief glare in his direction.

"Get in the car, Alana." He sped up a little, then pulled off to the side of the road and stepped out of the car.

"I said no." I took a step back as I stared at him.

"You're getting in the car. I'm going to drive you back to Oak Brook Academy because if you end up stranded out here somewhere in the middle of the night, then it's going to be me that gets in trouble for it."

"There is no way I'm getting in a car with you." I shook my head, then started to walk again.

"I'm sorry, okay?" He crossed his arms. "Sherry should have told you about the tradition. She's supposed to tell all the girls and if anyone has a problem with it, they let us know, so that this kind of thing doesn't happen. Mick asked Sherry and she told him that she'd told you."

"Shocking." I frowned. "It's a stupid tradition."

"Aren't most?" He shrugged. "Mick feels terrible. After he had such a good game, his night shouldn't end with him worrying about you getting home. Just let me help you out." He shifted closer to me. "Alana, he really didn't know."

I looked down the long road. I didn't even know if I was going in the right direction. Then I looked back at Graham.

"I want to go to Oak Brook, not back to the party."

"That's where I'll take you, I swear." He smiled.

"Alright." I sighed as I pulled open the passenger side door. It had already been a long day and a long night. I didn't want to get lost in the middle of the city. As I closed the door behind me, another set of headlights flashed into my eyes just before Graham pulled the car away from the curb.

"Music?" He turned the volume up on his radio.

I closed my eyes and leaned my head back against the seat. There was that headache again.

Graham pulled up outside the entrance of the school and looked over at me. "Can we keep all this between us? Or are you going to run to the principal?"

"I'm not going to run to the principal." I popped open the passenger door.

"I knew you would be cool, Alana." He leaned across the car and smiled at me. "I'm glad you're on the squad. And don't worry, from now on, I'll be keeping my eye on you."

"Thanks." I quirked an eyebrow as I studied him, then pushed the door closed. The last thing I wanted was Graham keeping his eye on me. It seemed like an odd thing for him to say.

As I trudged toward the girls' dormitory, I tried to piece together what had had happened exactly. Mick had been my in and now that was ruined. Maybe I'd overreacted. Maybe I should have played along. But it was too late now to change things.

I stepped into my dorm and closed the door behind me.

"What happened to you?" Cyndi gasped as she stood up from the sofa.

"I really don't want to talk about it." I shook my head as I headed for the bathroom. "I just want a shower and my bed."

"Sounds like things didn't go so well." She frowned as she followed after me.

"Cyndi." I paused at my bathroom door and turned to look at her. "I mean, I really don't want to talk about it."

"Got it."

I saw her back away from the door as I closed it behind me. I turned on the hot water in the shower.

Perhaps it was a good thing that Mick had turned out to be as much of a buffoon as the rest of the players. It meant that I had no reason to be distracted or to worry about the fallout from my story. Perhaps I'd thought there was something between us—when those sparks took my by surprise—but now I was certain it was all my imagination.

Maby might have a different opinion of Mick, but as far as I was concerned, he was just another pretty face in a jersey that cost more than the funds that the chess team received for the entire year.

That was what I needed to focus on.

NINE

Sunday morning I woke up to a pounding headache. Maybe it was from the tension of the day before or maybe it was from my inability to sleep soundly. I kept waking up throughout the night with a sensation that I'd forgotten something.

Annoyed, I climbed out of bed and prepared to spend my day as far away from Mick as I could. The memory of him pushing me into the water continued to play through my mind.

As I left my dorm room, I planned to spend some time in the library doing some research on the school's funds and how they were allocated, but before I could get past the common room, Maby caught me in the hallway.

"There you are." She smiled at me. "I hear you had quite an evening last night."

"I did." I crossed my arms.

"Mick christened you, huh?" She grinned.

"If that's what you want to call it. I did not enjoy it."

"Really?" Maby raised an eyebrow. "I thought you two were hitting it off pretty well?"

"I thought we were too—until he pushed me in the water."

"But you know that's just tradition, right? If the football

players win a game and are dating a cheerleader, they give her a push into the water to celebrate. Kind of like pouring the cooler over the coach." She laughed. "I think it's absurd, but then again, I'm not a cheerleader."

"Tradition or not, I didn't know about it and I didn't like it."

"Didn't someone tell you about it?" Maby narrowed her eyes.

"No. I never gave permission for it either." I shook my head. "I don't know what is going on in Mick's head, but that was too much for me." I started to walk through the common room.

"He's really not a bad guy, Alana." Maby fell into step beside me. "You just need to get to know him better."

I bit into my bottom lip. The truth was, I had begun to really like Mick—against my better judgment. But whether or not I liked him, he was much more than just a romantic interest. He was the key to getting the information that I needed.

"I'm sorry, Maby, I know you're good friends with him, but the way we left things last night was not positive."

"That's alright. Emotions were charged." She shrugged. "It doesn't mean you can't work it out today." She pushed open the door to the courtyard.

"I don't know. I have a lot of work to do. I'm going to the library." I paused on the top of the steps and turned to look at her. "I don't think he's a bad guy, but that doesn't mean we can get along."

"I know that." Maby sighed. "I always say, high school is not the place for romance. But the two of you just seem so perfect together, if you ask me."

"Sorry." I stared at her a moment longer, then walked in the direction of the library. Maybe if I refocused on my mission, I'd be able to ignore the nagging sensation inside me that I wasn't ready to give up on Mick. I told myself it was because he was my way in, but that didn't explain the butterflies that took flight in my stomach at the mere thought of his lips brushing against my ear.

"Ugh, stop it." I rolled my eyes and pushed through the door of the library.

Several heads turned to look at me. Only then did I realize that I'd mumbled my words out loud.

"Sorry. There was a bee." I cleared my throat and hurried to an empty computer.

As I logged in, I thought about what Maby had said. If Mick really did think that I'd given permission, could I blame him for shoving me into the pool? I wasn't sure. I also didn't know if I cared.

As I began to sort through the collection of bookmarks I'd already accumulated, I selected the football section. Yes, I had managed to get photographs of several receipts from purchases that the head coach had made with the school's funds. They amounted to thousands of dollars, and those were only the receipts that I'd been able to find.

I was lost in thought when I heard a chair pull up beside mine. I jumped at the sound and quickly turned off the monitor. A quick glance in the direction of the chair revealed Mick, his eyes locked on me and his lips set in a determined grimace.

"We need to talk."

"I don't have anything to say to you." I turned in my chair to face him, mostly to prevent him from seeing the collection of notes I'd spread out around me.

"Alana, you've got to believe me. I thought you wanted me to push you in the pool." He leaned forward and reached for my hands.

"No." I drew my hands back. "I don't have to believe you. I've never even heard of this ridiculous tradition, and if you had known me better, you would know that I never would have agreed to it." I raised an eyebrow. "But you don't know me, do you?"

"No, you're right, I don't." He looked intently at me as he scooted his chair closer. "But I want to get to know you. I want to know everything about you, Alana."

"Why?" I pushed my hair back over my shoulders. "There's no reason for you to be this interested in me."

"Aren't I the one that's supposed to decide that?" He smiled as he stared at me. "You're so tough, so sure of yourself. I like that about you, but you shouldn't let it keep people away from you."

"And by people, I assume you mean you?" I crossed my legs as I studied him. Why did he have to be so handsome? Why did I get so easily taken in by his warm brown eyes?

"I am a person." He nodded as he smiled.

"You think charm gets you out of everything, huh? Is that how it's always been for you?"

"You think you know me?" He tipped his head to the side. "I mean, I am charming. You can't argue with that."

"Playfulness is cute sometimes, Mick, but not everything can be laughed off." I turned back to the computer and began to gather up my notes.

"Alana, listen." He caught my hand by the wrist and met my eyes. "I don't want to laugh this off. I want a chance to make it up to you. Can you give me that?"

"What exactly does that mean?" My heart skipped a beat. Why was he trying so hard? Did he really have an interest in me?

"Just come with me this afternoon. I have somewhere I want to take you. Somewhere we can figure all this out." He trailed his fingertips along the inside of my wrist as he released my hand. "I just want a chance, that's it."

"Okay, fine. But to make things clear, I have no interest in being pushed, thrown, or picked up, okay?"

"Okay." He smiled as he stood up. "I'll meet you in the common room at noon."

"I'll be there." I nodded as I stood up as well.

"Oh, you dropped something." He picked up one of my notes from the floor, glanced at it, then handed it to me. "Are you writing a story on Coach?"

My cheeks flushed as I wondered how much he'd seen. "Something like that."

"Let me know if you need any help. I've got some great stories about that guy." He winked at me, then turned and walked out of the library.

As I stared after him, my grip tightened on my notes.

What if Mick really was interested in me? What if I really was interested in him? He wouldn't exactly be thrilled with the article I was writing. I pushed the thought from my mind. Finding the truth was what mattered the most. If that meant playing along with Mick's crush, that was what I would do. If that meant having to ignore the fact that I was starting to feel the same way about him, I'd have to do that too. I was convinced that I could handle it.

But by the time noon rolled around, I had tried on three different outfits and styled my hair in several different ways.

"Ugh!" I tossed my brush.

"You okay in there?" Cyndi called out from the living room.

"Fine." I tugged the hairband out of my hair and let it fall loose against my shoulders. There were plenty of things I could have done with that time, but I'd gotten caught up in the idea of looking nice for Mick.

"You look good." Cyndi smiled at me as I walked past her. "Meeting up with Mick?"

"Shush!" I waved to her over my shoulder.

"I knew it!" She laughed. "Good luck!"

"Thanks." I sighed as I closed the door.

Remember, Alana, this is business, this is about finding the truth, not losing yourself in big brown eyes.

I felt strong as I stepped into the common room, until I spotted him perched on the arm of one of the sofas. He looked relaxed in his t-shirt and jeans, but the moment he saw me, he straightened up and smiled.

"There you are." He offered me his arm. "Ready?"

"Ready for what exactly?" I wrapped my arm around his and clenched my jaw against the rush of excitement that his closeness inspired.

"You'll see." He pushed open the door of the common room and led me outside.

TEN

I tried to think of something to say as Mick led me through the courtyard and past the library. Everything that popped into my mind seemed silly or awkward. Maybe because I could hardly string two thoughts together while his hand was wrapped around mine. Why did my heart have to pound so hard? Would I even make it to this mystery location?

He glanced over at me and smiled. "Don't worry, it's not much further."

For a split-second I wondered if this whole thing might be a trick. I still didn't understand why Mick wanted my company so much. He claimed the pool was an accident, but was it?

"Where are we going?" I frowned. "We're almost off school grounds. I don't have permission to leave."

"We're not going to leave." He turned to face me. "Before I can take you any further, you have to make me a promise."

"What kind of promise?" I searched his eyes.

"What I'm about to reveal to you—it's a secret and sacred place. Only people who are worthy are ever allowed near it." He brushed a few strands of hair back behind my ear. "I know that you're more than worthy, but you still have to promise."

"This is silly." I rolled my eyes.

"Alana, I'm serious." He tightened his grasp on my hand. "Will you promise me that you will never tell anyone else about this place?"

I hesitated. I didn't like secrets. I didn't like making promises about things that I didn't fully understand. But the way he was looking at me made me think it was very important to him. And I had to admit that I was incredibly curious.

"I promise." I stared straight into his eyes.

"Good." He grinned, then tugged me forward. "Trust me, you're going to love it."

"Alright." I took a deep breath as he steered me between some buildings and into a nearly empty parking lot. An old boarded-up building stood off to the side. I felt a pinch of fear. "Mick, are you sure we're allowed to be here?"

"Define allowed." He chuckled as he pulled me forward. "Don't worry, we won't get in any trouble as long as we don't get caught."

"I don't want to get caught." I frowned as I sped up to match his pace. "Mick!"

"Shh!" He glanced at me, then pushed open the door to the old building.

"I don't want to go in there." I pulled back as my heart skipped a beat.

"It's alright." He stared at me. "You're not afraid of me, are you?"

"I don't even know you, Mick." I took a sharp breath.

"I think you know me better than you think." He stepped toward me. "We can go in together or we can sit out here all day together. I don't care. I just want to spend time with you. But I promise, this place is pretty amazing."

"Fine." I frowned as I studied him. "It better be good."

As a hint of excitement sparked within me, I reminded

myself that this was just business. This was just a way for me to get more information for my article. Mick might be charming, he might be handsome, he might even be a pretty good guy, but none of that mattered. I had to find a way to keep my distance, no matter what.

He stepped back through the door and led me in behind him.

I expected a dusty old room full of mouse droppings and maybe some broken tools. Instead, I found what amounted to a strange paradise. From curtains draped across the walls to piles of cushions spread in every direction, I realized that this place was more than just a hideaway. It had been painted and filled with luxurious items.

"What is this place?" I laughed a little as he pulled back a silk curtain.

"It's a special place." He pulled me down on the pile of cushions.

"Hey! Watch it!" I frowned as I met his eyes. "Didn't I tell you about pushing me?"

"I pulled." His eyes widened. "And only because I wanted to show you this." He pointed up at the ceiling.

"Wow!" I sprawled back and drank in the sight of the ceiling. It had been painted with a mural that depicted mountains, waterfalls, distant stars, and what I thought might be a unicorn. "Did you paint this?"

"Me?" He laughed. "No. That's Apple's special talent."

"Apple." I nodded. "She's one of your friends, right?"

"Yes. There's Maby, Apple, Fi, Candy, Chuckles, and Wes. We all share this space. And now you do too." He rose up on his elbow as he looked at me. "I wanted you to see that there's more to me than just football."

"I know that."

"Do you?" He leaned a little closer. "I thought that maybe

we could get to know each other a little better here—where it's quiet, where there aren't any distractions."

"You mean, you just wanted to get me alone?" I grinned and tossed one of the pillows at him.

"No!" He caught it mid-air and tucked it under his elbow. "I mean that I want to share something that's special to me with someone who is special to me."

"Special to you?" I tipped my head to the side. "How can I be special when you don't know anything about me?"

"I don't know." He smiled as he studied me. "There's just something there, something that I can't look away from. Besides, I think I might know more about you than you think."

"Why? Has Maby blabbed?" I couldn't help but smile in return. His sweet words combined with his smooth voice made me feel at ease. But the moment my heart began to speed up, I reminded myself that this was just a way to get information. It couldn't be anything more than that. I had no idea what made Mick fixate on me, but whatever it was, I had to keep playing into it, at least until my article was done.

"Not at all." He rolled his eyes, then grinned. "Well, maybe a little. Just how much she likes you. I asked her about bringing you here, you know."

"You did?"

"Yes. I thought it would be the respectful thing to do. She couldn't wait for me to do it."

"Maby is a good friend." I stretched out on the cushions, then looked up at the ceiling again. "I had no idea that Apple was so artistic. She never says too much about herself."

"She's shy. Painfully shy. I've tried to break her out of it, but she just gets even more shy." He sat up and looked over at me. "I think you'll like her when you get to know her."

"I'd like that." I sat up as well and pulled my knees up to my chest. "Thanks for bringing me here, Mick. It was very kind of you."

"Does this mean I'm forgiven?" He scooted closer to me on the cushions.

"Forgiven?" I eyed him and shook my head. "It's going to take a lot more than a secret hideaway to get me to forgive you for shoving me into a pool."

"What about catching you when you fell off the bleachers?" He raised an eyebrow. "That should count for something."

"You're right." I stroked his cheek without even thinking about it. As my fingertips coasted along his skin, my breath slowed. A slow shiver swam up along my spine. There it was again, that undeniable reaction to being close to him. "I guess maybe we can call it even."

He caught my hand and pressed it against his cheek as he gazed into my eyes. Then he leaned forward, his lips aimed for mine.

"Slow down." I ducked my head out of the way and took a sharp breath.

"I'm sorry." He frowned as he drew back. "I guess I read that wrong. I thought maybe it was the right moment."

"Mick." I created a little more distance between us. "Look, I'm sure you're used to things moving fast, but I need to get to know you before things go any further. If that's not what you're interested in, I understand."

"I'm interested in you, Alana." He took my hand and stroked his thumb along the back of it. "However that comes, however you need things to be, I'm interested in you."

ELEVEN

I stared into his eyes as my mind spun. Had he really just said that to me? There wasn't a hint of laughter in his voice. Was he serious?

"Mick, I'm not sure—"

"Who's in here?" a voice bellowed from the doorway.

Mick jumped up to his feet and peered around the curtain at the door. "It's just me, Chuckles."

"Sorry, Mick, I didn't know you were here. I heard voices." Chuckles stepped past the curtain. He settled his gaze on me, then looked back at Mick. "Really?"

"I got Maby's permission."

"Okay." Chuckles looked at me again. "Welcome, I guess."

"I'm Alana." I offered him my hand as I stood up.

"Oh, that's not going to work." He grinned as he scanned me from my head to my toes. "Nobody gets away with a real name around here."

"Except Wes?" Mick crossed his arms.

"Wes is still a nickname. If she's going to be welcomed in, she's got to have a new name." He shrugged. "It's not my rule."

"Sometimes people call me Lani…" I raised an eyebrow.

"Too easy." Chuckles pointed his finger at me. "Don't worry, I'll think of something."

"Sounds scary," I muttered as Chuckles continued further into the building.

"Maby and the others are on their way. Looks like your alone time is going to be interrupted." He turned back to look at us. "Sorry, kids." He grinned, then disappeared through another door.

"Kids?" I smiled.

"Chuckles thinks he's the adult around here because he's seventeen." Mick rolled his eyes. "It's easier just to let him feel important."

"Maybe I should go." I watched the door. "It feels a little invasive for me to be here."

"Not at all. Maby gave her approval. It's better if you get to know everyone now, because once you're invited in, it's like being part of a family."

I bit into my bottom lip. I'd made friends during my time at Oak Brook, but not close ones. Being invited into a group—one that acted like family—it sounded really good to me. But wasn't it all based on a lie?

I glanced over at Mick as he straightened up the cushions we'd used. The moment I looked at him, warmth brewed within me. Okay, maybe it wasn't a complete lie.

"Alana!" Maby called out as she swept in through the door with Candy and Apple. She wrapped her arms around me and squeezed. "I'm so glad you're here."

"I hear I have you to thank for this." I smiled as I hugged her back. "Thanks for the approval."

"Oh, it wasn't just me. The way that Mick talks about you—well, I couldn't possibly turn him down." She leaned closer and whispered. "He has it bad for you, Alana." As she straightened up she looked directly into my eyes. "You'd better not break his heart."

Something about her tone and her expression sent an icy jolt through my body. I'd never seen her look so serious. What exactly would she do to me if I did happen to break his heart? My stomach twisted at the thought.

"Go easy on her, Maby. You're going to scare her off." Candy gave Maby a light slap on the shoulder. "Don't worry, Alana, we all know how fickle Mick is. You'll be lucky if he doesn't break your heart." Candy flopped down on the cushions and yawned. "Isn't that right, Mick?"

"I'm not fickle." He crossed his arms.

"Yes, you are." Apple flashed him a smile as she brushed past me.

"Apple, right?" I tried to catch her eye. "You're the one who painted the ceiling?"

"Yup, that's me." She avoided looking at me but smiled a little.

"It's beautiful. You're very talented. Are you in the arts program?" I again tried to meet her eyes.

"Uh, I'm working on it." She cleared her throat.

"She won't submit her work." Candy pursed her lips. "If she did, she'd be in it in a second, but she won't do it."

"Shut up, Candy!" Apple threw a pillow at her. "It's hard enough keeping up with the classwork here."

"You can handle it." Candy threw the pillow back at her.

"Enough." Mick caught the pillow in mid-air. "Apple does things her own way, in her own time, right, Apple?"

"Right." Apple smiled at him. "Thanks, Mick."

I smiled as well. I liked seeing Mick come to Apple's defense.

"Well, you certainly have the talent for it." I turned back to Maby. "This place is great. I had no idea it was here."

"Good, we need to keep it that way. It gives us a space away from the rest of the crowd." Maby sprawled out on the cushions. "Sometimes a place like Oak Brook can be nothing but pressure. Here, we don't have to deal with it."

"At least we try not to." Mick crossed the room to reach my side. He draped his arm around my shoulders. "You should see this one out on the field. Wow! Never seen anyone move like that."

"I'll bet." Maby smiled as she looked up at me. "I'll leave the school athletics to you two. I'm not much of a joiner. But I do like to watch Mick play. Did you know there are some scouts already looking at him, Alana?"

"Really?" I glanced over at him, fully aware of the warmth and weight of his arm around me. "That's pretty impressive."

"Eh, it doesn't mean anything. Everyone on the team is super talented." He shrugged. "We'll see what happens at the end of the year. Talk about pressure. Coach Baker has been all over me this year."

"How do you handle that?" I tentatively wrapped my arm around his waist to draw him closer.

"Mostly I just ignore him." He frowned. "Sometimes it gets to me, though. He can be really rough on some of the guys. I liked Coach Jackson way better."

"He left last year, right?" I tipped my head to the side as I studied him. The truth was, I knew a lot about Coach Jackson's departure.

"Yeah, that was a shock." He sighed, then shook his head. "Anyway, I don't want to talk about that. Where are Wes and Fi?"

"Oh, they're out prancing through the flowers somewhere." Candy rolled her eyes. "So happy and in love."

"Candy, don't be bitter." Maby shot her a look.

"I'm not trying to be bitter, but don't you think they could be just a little less cutesy about it? I mean, Wes?" She cringed. "He's changed."

"He's in love." Mick smiled. "You can't blame a man for being changed by that." His arm tightened around my shoulders. "I'm happy for them both."

"Me too." Candy sighed. "I just don't need my nose rubbed in it."

"Don't worry, Candy." Mick looked at her. "The right person is going to come along for you too."

"Oh please, we're all in high school, there are no right people." Maby sat up and looked straight at Mick. "The most you can hope for is someone to make life a little more exciting until we get out into the real world."

"I don't know about that." Mick murmured as he glanced at me. "I think sometimes you get lucky."

My skin buzzed with excitement as he stared into my eyes with a heat that I hadn't seen before. Was that passion? My heart skipped a beat as he leaned closer. Did he intend to kiss me—right there in front of everyone?

Instead, he trailed his hand back through my hair and smiled. "Maybe we should prance through some of those flowers, huh?"

"I actually have a lot of homework to do." I stammered.

"She has homework, Mick!" Maby burst out laughing. "You're such a bad influence."

"I am not." He grinned. "Stick with me, Lala, and I'll get you out of all your homework." He winked.

"Lala?" I cringed.

"I like it." Maby nodded. "It's approved."

"What about Lani?" I looked between the two of them.

"Lala has a nice ring to it." Candy nodded.

"I like it too." Apple smiled.

"It's decided then." Maby grinned. "Lala it is."

"I'll take you back." Mick tugged me out through the door. Once outside, he pulled me close and whispered. "Lala, because I hear music every time I see you."

I pulled back and looked straight at him. Again, there was no hint of amusement in his eyes.

My heart pounded as I began to realize that Mick wasn't playing games or pranks. He meant every word he said. This beautiful person really did seem to be interested in me—maybe even falling for me?

TWELVE

Though the nickname felt silly, I couldn't ignore the fact that the way he described it filled me with warmth. No one had ever seen me that way, no one had ever said these kinds of things to me. I slipped my hand into his as we walked back toward the dormitories.

"What got you started playing football, Mick?"

"Actually, I started when I was about eight. I hated it." He winced. "I used to get so mad every time my mom made me go to practice."

"Why did she make you if you didn't want to go?" I frowned.

"At the time, I had no idea. But every week she'd drop me off at practice for a few hours and I'd have to endure it. It wasn't long before I started to realize that I was bigger than most of the other kids. When I practiced, I was better too. I started to like it." He drew a deep breath. "Later, I found out that my mom took me to practice every week because she had taken on extra hours to make ends meet. My dad wasn't around much and she needed to make up the difference."

"Oh wow, I'm sorry to hear that. That must have been hard on both of you." I tightened my grasp on his hand.

"I didn't really know any different. Then she met my stepfather. He was actually my football coach when I was ten. They hit it off and then his business took off. We went from barely getting by to having more than we could ever want." He smiled as he looked at me. "A real rags to riches story, huh?"

"It sounds like it. But I know things are never that simple. You kept playing football?" I shifted a little closer to him.

"Yes, my stepdad continued to coach me—that's how I ended up here. He heard the athletics program here was one of the best, so he made sure I could get in." He shrugged. "Sometimes, I think about that old football field I used to play on and the way I hated getting dropped off there. I wonder what would have happened if I'd kept fighting it?" He met my eyes. "Sometimes life has its own plans. You can try to fight it but then you might miss out on something great."

"We're not talking about football anymore, are we?" I stared at him.

"No. I don't want to talk about football. I want to talk about you." He smiled. "Tell me something that no one else knows."

"Mick, I think you're sweet." I drew my hand out of his and took a slight step back. "I really do. But this is all a little fast, don't you think? I mean, we still barely know each other."

"Because you keep avoiding my questions." He quirked an eyebrow. "The thing is, I'm the type of person that goes all-in. If I see something I want, I'm going to do everything I can to get it." He caught my hand again and held it, despite a subtle tug from me. "I'm not chasing you, that's not what I mean. I just mean, when I say that I'm interested in you and what we could be together, I'm being honest. I'm ready to do what it takes to see where this goes. If I come on a little strong, I'm sorry, it's just my nature. When I see someone as amazing as you, I'm not going to just step back and let you disappear. Like I said, we can take our time." He shrugged. "But as long as you don't tell me to leave you alone, you're going to have all of me."

All of him? I fought back a rush of desire as he leaned his head closer to mine and I detected the scent of his cologne. I wanted to throw my arms around him and pull him in for a kiss. I wanted him to sweep me up in his arms and tell me that no matter how confusing all this was, it would all make sense soon enough.

Instead, I closed my eyes.

"It's too much, isn't it?" he whispered.

I felt his fingertips trace the curve of my cheek. His palm settled on the slope of my neck as he stepped closer. "You can tell me to go anytime you want."

"I don't want you to." The words were spoken even before I had the chance to think of them. "Mick." I squeezed his hand. "I just need you to be patient."

"Always." He let his hand fall away. "Look at me, Lala."

I grinned at the nickname and shook my head as I opened my eyes. "That's ridiculous."

"It's not, it's beautiful." He laughed. "You're stuck with it now."

"It's all your fault." I gave him a playful shove.

"Yes, that's true." He looped his arm through mine as we continued to walk toward the dormitories.

As the sun began to set in the sky, I realized that I loved every moment that we'd spent together that afternoon. I loved the way he touched me when I least expected it, I loved his laughter, and most of all, I loved his determination to be with me.

What could there be about me that had him so wrapped up?

"Mick, you said you know more about me than I think. What do you mean by that?"

"I might be a little bit of a stalker." He winced as he smiled.

"Huh?" I laughed.

"Not in a bad way. It's just—I've been reading your articles in the school newspaper all year. I love that you leave the flowery stuff out of it and you just get down to the real information. I had no idea that there was such a trash issue on school grounds until that article you did. Since then, I've been making an effort to recycle more and use less."

"You actually read that?" I grinned. "I didn't think anyone did."

"I did. I've read all your articles." He tipped his head from side to side. "I don't always agree with all of them, but I always enjoy them."

"Oh, let me guess, you didn't like the one I wrote about the football players getting out of detention after that prank you guys pulled earlier this year?" I raised an eyebrow as I stopped in front of the dormitories.

"It wasn't very flattering, no." He leaned close to my ear, so close that I could feel the warmth of his breath tickle along my skin. "You don't know the whole story."

"You could always tell me." I touched his chest lightly as he lingered close to me. "I could write a new article—with new information."

"You'd like that, wouldn't you?" He brushed my hair back along my shoulder, his fingertips grazing my neck as he did. "You want me to tell you all my secrets, don't you?" He leaned back enough to look into my eyes.

"I'm willing to listen." My heart skipped a beat as we shared our breath, just a few inches of space between us. "Whenever you want to confess."

"Who says I have anything to confess?" He searched my eyes.

His hand settled on my shoulder. With just a light tug he

could bring my lips to his. I felt a crackle in the air between us that awakened my senses in a brand new way.

"Do you?" I slid my hand from his chest to the back of his neck and gazed up at him. "What are you hiding behind all that charm?"

"I don't hide." He inched just a little closer.

I wondered if he could smell the peach scent of my lip gloss. Could he sense that heat billowed through me and it was taking all my resistance not to kiss him?

"Not ever? Not from anyone?" I smiled as I felt a faint shiver course through him underneath my palm.

"Never." His hand slipped from the curve of my shoulder to the back of my neck.

My heart raced. This was it. This was the moment that he would kiss me. I didn't care about anything but how soft and sweet his lips would be.

I lifted up a little on my toes and tilted my mouth toward his.

"I don't chase either." His lips just missed mine and landed on my cheek. They lingered there just long enough for the touch to be considered a kiss, then he leaned back as he smiled. "I promised I'd be patient, Lala, and I meant that. When you're ready, all you have to do is let me know."

I thought about telling him that I was ready right that second as a flood of disappointment washed over me. My cheeks flushed. Did he know that I had intended to kiss him? Did I look like a fool?

"I will." I managed to mumble the words.

"Good." He ran his hand down my arm to my hand and gave it a light squeeze. "I'll see you at practice tomorrow?"

"I'll be there." I nodded, then in a daze, I walked into the dormitory.

I couldn't make sense of what had just happened. He'd been

reading my work since I started writing for the paper? He liked me because of who I was, not just because I was some random girl that had sparked his interest? I hadn't expected that or the way that it made me feel.

As I sprawled out in bed that night, my heart continued to pound.

Maybe Mick wasn't the only one falling in love.

THIRTEEN

I woke up the next morning with a faint smile on my lips. Strange sensations flowed through me from head to toe. Happiness? Excitement? I curled my toes and closed my eyes. How could Mick have such an impact on me?

When I opened my eyes again, I realized that it was still dark. I glanced at the clock on my bedside table. Why had I set the alarm so early?

My mind spun for a few seconds, then I remembered the reason. Today was the day that I graduated from investigative journalist to investigative spy. I needed more information and the best way to get it was from the source.

I climbed out of bed and dressed quietly. I didn't need Cyndi asking me questions. The less people who knew about my activities, the better.

I slipped out of my dorm room, down the hall, and through the common room. Everything was quiet. The lights were dim. Was this the magical time of day when everyone actually slept at the same time? I hoped so, because getting into the athletics office undetected would depend on its being empty.

As I walked across the courtyard, I found the absence of

laughter and activity to be a little eerie. Usually the area was packed with young and eager souls looking to get and give attention.

I thought about being surrounded by friends the day before, about Mick's revealing his secret hideout to me and inviting me into his world. It was lovely to feel as if I belonged. But did I really?

When they found out what I was actually up to, everything would change.

I reached the athletics building parking lot. Not a single car filled a space. My heartbeat quickened. If I had a chance to get inside before Coach Baker did, I might be able to find some paperwork or something else to indicate that he was fully aware of the discrepancies in his purchases.

The receptionist for the office was not in yet, which made it easy for me to walk through the reception area and down the hall to the athletic offices. Coach Baker had the largest office in the corner of the building. As I got closer to it, I noticed that the door was slightly open. A bicycle leaned against the wall in the hallway.

I winced. Not everyone drove cars to work, apparently.

The glass windows in the office allowed me to see Coach Baker inside as well as a student—a student I recognized right away.

"Mick?" I took a sharp breath as I ducked back to avoid being seen. I'd walked into a hornet's nest, not just at risk of Coach Baker's catching me sneaking around, but how would I explain my presence to Mick?

My chest ached at the thought of the look on his face when I admitted to trying to take down the entire football team. Maybe he would find a way to forgive me, but I doubted it.

I held my breath as the voices in the office became louder.

"Ty is a great quarterback, I'm just saying I think you should play him more." Mick's voice sounded persuasive. "He's always sitting on the bench. He's never going to be picked up by a recruiter if he doesn't get to play."

"So, you're questioning my decisions as a coach?" Coach Baker's terse tone echoed through the empty hallway.

"I'm just saying—could it really hurt that much to put him in now and then?"

"That's not how we operate around here, Mick."

I narrowed my eyes as I wondered what he meant by that. Why wouldn't he put a talented player on the field? What could be holding him back?

"Because he's on scholarship, right?" Mick's tone darkened. "That's why you keep him on the bench."

"Again you're questioning me." Coach Baker's voice hardened. "Maybe you need a reminder of just how important I am in your life, Mick?"

I took a sharp breath. Was he threatening Mick? My thoughts raced. Could Coach Baker really get away with talking to one of his star players like that?

"I know how important you are." Mick's voice softened. "I just thought—"

"That's your first problem." Coach Baker chuckled. "I'm the one that does the thinking around here, remember? It's what they pay me for. Your job is to make the school look good by winning games, not to play hero to some poor kid that's already won the lottery just by being here. He's getting an education he couldn't have dreamed about before he got into Oak Brook Academy. That should be enough."

"I'm not trying to be a hero, Coach, I'm really not." Mick cleared his throat. "But you said it's my job to make the school look good, and I think putting Ty in for a few games would make it look great. I think together we could really rack up some wins."

"Sorry, pal, you know that's not how this works." Coach Baker's voice lowered, but it got sterner. "You win out there, because that is your job. You don't need any special help. If you do need help, that's a problem we need to discuss. Is it, Mick? Is it a problem for you to go out there and bring home the wins that you owe me?"

"No, Coach." Mick sighed. "It's not a problem."

"Are you sure?"

"I'm sure. Forget I said anything. It was stupid."

"Yes, it was." Coach Baker laughed. "Let's forget about all of it, alright?"

"You've got it, Coach." Mick's voice grew louder as the two stepped out into the hallway.

I flattened myself against the wall. There weren't many other options. If the two came around the corner, I'd be caught and everything I'd just heard that tied my stomach into knots would be known.

"Did you take up the collection this week?" Coach Baker's voice sounded a little further away.

I felt some relief as I realized that they were headed in the other direction down the hallway. A quick peek around the corner revealed that Coach Baker had left the door to his office wide open. This was my chance to get inside. But my mind was fixated on the conversation I'd just overheard. What did it all mean? It seemed to me that Mick would do whatever Coach Baker asked him to, but why?

"Yeah, I've got it all," Mick replied, his voice a little more distant.

I peeked around the corner again and caught sight of them near an exit door.

As I watched, Mick pulled an envelope out of his pocket and held it out to Coach Baker. "I made sure."

"Good job." Coach Baker took the envelope and lifted the

flap. He ran his thumb across a stack of cash, then closed the envelope again. "I've always said that you have a bright future." He smiled as he looked at Mick. "Do me a favor, don't prove me wrong, alright?"

"I won't, Coach." Mick shoved his hands in his pockets.

"No more thinking." Coach Baker tapped his fingertip lightly against Mick's forehead. "That can get you into all kinds of trouble. You don't want trouble, do you, Mick?"

"No, sir." Mick lowered his head and took a slight step back.

"Good. Now, get out there and do some sprints before class starts. Your speed has been dropping lately." He pushed open the exit door. "On the double!"

"Yes, Coach." Mick pushed past him and out the door.

Coach Baker stepped out after him.

I stood in the hallway, stunned by what I'd seen.

Why had Mick given him an envelope full of cash? Why did Coach Baker continue to imply that Mick needed to do everything he told him to?

As much as I didn't want to believe it, I realized that my investigation no longer centered just around Coach Baker and the rest of the coaching staff, but also around Mick, who appeared to be in the middle of everything. I thought I'd stumbled across a school administration favoring one team over the rest, but now it seemed there was much more to it than just that.

I stared at the open door of the office. Now, more than ever, I had to find out exactly what was going on with Coach Baker. I glanced once over my shoulder to be sure that no one had entered the building behind me, then I crossed the distance to the office door.

This was it. If I were caught now, I'd have no way of talking my way out of it.

FOURTEEN

The office smelled like footballs and grass. I noticed a pile of paperwork on the desk. As I picked up the piece of paper on top, I read through a list of players' names. Mick's was included. Ty's was not. Beside it were dollar amounts that I didn't understand.

I snapped a picture of the piece of paper, which had notes from Coach Baker across the bottom. I set the paper back down and picked up another. This one listed the team's finances. I snapped a picture of that.

Then I moved on to a third piece of paper. This one appeared to be a request for more funds from the school administration. My stomach twisted at the thought of the football team's receiving even more money. I snapped a picture of it, then heard a door slam. I jumped at the sound.

Footsteps carried down the hall in my direction. It sounded like they came from the exit door at the end of the hallway. There was no time to get out the door of the office. I hid in the only place available—underneath the desk.

I held my breath as the footsteps continued into the office. I saw Coach Baker's shoes on the other side of the desk. In mere seconds he would walk around it and attempt to sit down in his chair, only to discover me hiding there.

I tried to think of an excuse for my presence, but nothing made sense. I heard a low whistle, another rustling of papers, and then more footsteps. Only this time they walked away from the desk, toward the door of the office. Seconds later they continued down the hall.

I had no way of knowing exactly where he was in the hallway, but I didn't want to give him the time to come back. I had to get out while I could.

I bolted out from under the desk, rushed out of the office and ran down the hall to the exit door. Whether he heard or saw me or not, I had no idea, as I was already on the other side of the door before I even took a breath.

In the distance, I saw Mick running sprints across the football field. He was alone out there.

I could go out there and question him. I could demand to know why he'd handed cash to Coach Baker. I could ask him about the coach's threats.

My heart sank at the thought.

Mick, whom I'd just begun to think could be more than just a friend, was now a suspect in my book. I wanted him to be innocent. I wanted there to be an explanation. But what if there wasn't? What if what I heard was true.

Mick and Coach Baker had something going on between them, something that benefited both of them. And something that I assumed couldn't be legal or morally right. Whatever it was, it kept Ty on a bench instead of on the field where he belonged, and Mick had agreed to that.

Everything I thought I knew about him fled my mind. I'd fallen for his charm, for that pretty smile and those sweet words. Of course he was a con artist. He and Coach Baker were up to something together. He knew how to play people, how to manipulate them, and I was just another person to conquer.

Anger rushed through me as I thought about how foolish I'd been. I'd actually believed that he was interested in me. I'd actually believed that he saw something in me that he didn't see in anyone else. I'd let my desire for him cloud my judgment.

As I walked away from the football field, a darker thought settled into my mind. Mick said he'd been watching me for a while. He'd read my articles. He had an idea of what I was up to. What if the only reason he'd even shown an interest in me was to get a better idea of what I was investigating?

By the time I reached my first class, my stomach was in knots. Not only did I feel like an idiot for falling for Mick, now I wondered if I was even capable of being the investigative reporter that I hoped to be one day. If I could be so easily fooled, did I have the instincts for it?

At lunch, to get my mind off of Mick, I focused on the pictures I'd taken of the paperwork on Coach Baker's desk. I'd begun to zoom in on one of them when Maby sat down beside me.

"Hey, Lala." She flashed me a grin.

"It's Alana." I closed the picture before she could see it.

"Sorry, you're stuck with Lala now." She nudged my shoulder with her own. "I'm so glad that you and Mick are hitting it off. I can totally see the two of you together."

"Can you?" I tilted my head to the side and smiled.

"Absolutely. Mick's such a sweet person and he would treat you well. You're so smart and funny, you could certainly keep him entertained." She took a sip of her lemonade. "Why don't you make it official?"

"Make it official?"

"You've got to put it out there that he's taken so the girls will stop buzzing around him." She flicked her hand through the air. "We can't risk that, can we?"

"I don't know if we're quite ready for that." I frowned. I didn't know if I'd ever be able to look into Mick's eyes again without thinking about him handing Coach Baker that envelope full of money. But if I cut things off now, that would change everything. It would mean that my access to information about the football team would be limited and I might not ever figure out what was really going on.

Maybe Mick was playing me. Could I really blame him for that? I was playing him too—at least I had been to start with. If I hadn't let myself get so distracted by the warmth of his eyes and the way he looked at me, I never would have let things get so out of control.

I just needed to get back to that space where I saw Mick as an opportunity, not a romantic interest. If I could do that, then maybe I could still salvage the investigation and my friendship with Maby.

"Well, I wouldn't wait too long." Maby lowered her voice. "Mick's a pretty popular guy."

"I know." I frowned as I opened my bottle of water. "Do you know anything about another player on the team—Ty?"

"Ty? He's a friend of Mick's. He's a good guy. I don't know much about him though." She shrugged. "I know Mick is always complaining about how little he gets to play."

"Are they good friends?"

"I don't think so." Maby frowned. "It's hard to say. Mick sticks to our group pretty much, but he does spend a lot of time with his football buddies during the season. You're better off asking him." She took a bite of her sandwich, then met my eyes. "You're not going to play hard to get, are you? Mick isn't smart enough for that."

"I'm sure he is." I laughed, then shook my head. "No, I'm

not going to play hard to get, not at all. I think Mick is great." I swallowed back a few more opinions I had about him.

As far as Maby knew, I was in it for real, and that was all she ever needed to know. For the moment, I would continue to play into Mick's affections. I just had to make sure that I didn't lose myself in it again, that I didn't take it all so seriously.

As lunch ended, I felt a rush of determination. Yes, Coach Baker was up to something and I would find out what it was, even if that meant I had to use Mick to get to the truth.

I had practice that afternoon at the same time as the football players. It would be the first test of whether I could maintain my resolve.

Still, as I walked to my next class, I couldn't ignore a small part of me that hoped that maybe, just maybe, there was some kind of explanation for everything.

Maybe that ache in my heart would disappear.

FIFTEEN

After the last class, I headed out to the field.

Cheerleading practice. Something that I thought I would be thrilled to attend when I'd first started at the school, but now, I dreaded it.

Yes, the routines were fun, but the cold shoulder from the other cheerleaders wasn't—not to mention the fact that I would likely end up face to face with Mick. Could I really pretend that I was okay? That I had no idea what had happened that morning between him and Coach Baker?

I knew in the future, if I did decide to become a journalist, I might have to pretend in a similar way. But this time, in this situation, it wasn't just a story I was investigating. Just a look from Mick sent my heart racing.

I took a deep breath, then strode onto the field. Several cheerleaders looked in my direction and none of them smiled. I searched for the one friendly face I could count on. Hallie. But I couldn't find her in the crowd. Instead, I found Sherry, who glared at me with her hands on her hips.

"Nice of you to join us."

"Practice is at three-thirty, right?" I glanced at my watch.

"If practice is at three-thirty, then you need to be here by three." Sherry crossed her arms.

"Maybe if you'd told me that, I could have been here on time." I offered a smile. "I certainly wouldn't want to do anything to upset you."

"I shouldn't have to tell you. You should just know." Sherry turned on her heel and started to walk away.

"You mean, like I should have known about the tradition of the football players pushing cheerleaders into the pool after a big win?" I watched as she froze. "In fact, someone told me that Mick was assured I knew about and agreed to the tradition. But I didn't."

"Maybe you should worry less about traditions and more about what you're doing to the people around you." Sherry turned back to face me. "We'll be bringing on a new cheerleader next practice to replace one I had to let go."

"What are you talking about?" I narrowed my eyes.

"Hallie." She smirked, then bounded off across the field to the practice area.

The other cheerleaders followed her.

My heart sank. Hallie? Had I gotten her kicked off the team because she was friendly to me?

My blood boiled as I watched Sherry flip across the grass. She knew exactly what she was up to. She wanted to drive me to quit. But it wouldn't work. I was far more determined than that.

I ran after her and began to flip across the field as well. If she did two cartwheels, I did three. If she did a back flip, I did a back flip into a front flip into a spin.

As thrilling as it was to show her up, my body ached with pain by the time practice was over. Muscles that I hadn't used in a long time screamed with fury at my abuse. From the way Sherry limped off the field, I guessed that she had been pushing herself as well. As much as I hated to admit it, she did have some skill.

As the other cheerleaders cleared the field, I took a moment to breathe. It still broke my heart to think that Hallie had been thrown off the team because of me. Clearly Sherry wanted to hurt me in any way she could. But that was all the more reason not to let her get to me.

"It looks like you might need this."

I spotted the bottle of water before I realized who had offered it to me. When I looked up at him, I didn't have a second to prepare myself. Mick and those beautiful eyes were right in front of me and I'd forgotten that I needed to find a way to shield myself against his charm.

"Thanks." I took the bottle of water and hoped that he didn't notice the tremble in my hand.

"You were killing it out there." He smiled as he studied me.

"Killing might be the right word." I groaned as I rubbed the cold water bottle along my forearm.

"Sore?" His hand followed the path of the water bottle and rubbed at the tight muscles under my sweat-covered skin.

"Yes." I bit into my bottom lip as the warmth of his touch and the deep pressure of his fingertips threatened to break down all my defenses.

"You deserve a hot meal after all that hard work. I'm going to make you dinner tonight." He continued to work through the tension in my arm.

"Oh no, that's okay." I smiled. "I'll be fine." I pulled my arm free of his touch.

Remember the envelope, I reminded myself. *Remember that he isn't who he pretends to be.*

"I know you will be, because I'll be there to make sure you are. Trust me, I'm a good cook. My mother taught me well." He grinned. "I'll be there by six. I need a shower first."

Stop thinking about him in the shower, Alana.

I took a sharp breath as I wondered if that thought was shouted only in my mind—or had it slipped past my lips? From his lingering smile, I guessed that it hadn't.

But he knew, didn't he? I could see the glimmer of amusement in his eyes as he stared at me.

"Mick, you know you're not allowed in the girl's dormitory." I shook my head as I tried to gather my strength. I focused on the memory of Coach Baker speaking to him as if he owned him, as if Mick would do anything that he asked him to do.

"I have my ways." He murmured his words as he stepped closer to me. "What's wrong? Don't you want me to be there?"

My heart pounded as his closeness reminded me of just how much I wanted to kiss him the night before. Why did he have such an effect on me? It was as if he had crawled under my skin and tickled it from the inside just with the sound of his voice.

"Of course I do." I swallowed back my fear. Being alone with him would be difficult, but it would also give me the opportunity to probe him for more information about his relationship with Coach Baker. I couldn't turn that down. "I just don't want you to get in trouble because of me."

"Too late." He stroked my cheek and smiled. "I'm in plenty of trouble already." He winked at me, then jogged off across the field.

I did my best to keep myself steady as a rush of dizziness washed over me in reaction to his touch.

"Enough, Alana." I rolled my eyes, cracked open the bottle of water, and drank it down in a few swallows.

It was dehydration. That was all it was. I'd pushed myself so hard on the field that I couldn't think straight. It had nothing to do with any feelings I might have for Mick. Those feelings didn't matter, because the truth was, he was likely just as guilty as Coach Baker.

Luckily by the time I reached the locker room, most of the girls were gone, but a few still lingered. I could hear them talking from the next aisle over as I changed.

"I can't believe she would do that to Hallie."

"Really? I can. Sherry can be vicious."

"Shh! Don't talk about her like that—do you want to be next?"

"It's all Alana's fault anyway. Whatever she did to get on the squad pissed Sherry off. As long as she's around, none of us will be safe."

"She doesn't have to be around. She's a show-off anyway. Did you see her out there today? So maybe we're not all gymnasts. She doesn't have to rub it in."

"What are you saying?"

"I'm saying we should all help Sherry out. We need to make Alana quit, so that things can get back to normal."

"It's not like normal was good either."

I winced as I picked up my backpack. If the entire squad intended to target me, then it would be far more difficult for me to stick around. I had to find a way to get the target off my back. It certainly wouldn't help to give the cold shoulder to Mick.

With this on my mind, I headed back to the dormitory. It wouldn't be long before Mick arrived and I wanted to be ready to face him this time.

SIXTEEN

I stepped into my dorm room to find the living room empty.

"Cyndi?"

After receiving no response, I noticed a note on the counter in the kitchenette.

WENT out to give you and Mick some alone time. Have fun!

I STARED down at the note and took a slow breath. Alone with Mick? I glanced around the living room. Usually it looked like a pretty innocent room. But as I studied it, I noticed just how small the sofa was, the candles scattered all over the place, and the easy access to any music we might want to enjoy.

It was a trap, a trap that I was likely to get caught in if I didn't get my head on straight.

After a quick shower, I chose the frumpiest clothes I could find—an old pair of sweatpants and a baggy t-shirt from last year's relay race. I left my hair wet and stringy around my shoulders. I wouldn't do anything to encourage Mick's attraction.

Maybe that would allow me to resist my attraction to him. Maybe not.

I stared into the mirror, into the reflection of my own eyes. "Alana, you cannot screw this up."

My heart jolted at the sound of a knock on the door. For a split-second I considered not answering it. Would he just go away? Could I get away with that? The more I thought about it, the better it sounded.

During the second set of knocks, I held my breath. I wasn't just a girl avoiding a boy, I was a reporter avoiding a story. Maybe my hesitation had less to do with not wanting to get swept up in my feelings for Mick and more to do with my not wanting to discover the truth. It was easier for me to pretend that what I'd witnessed that morning had never happened than to face the fact that I had feelings for someone who was involved in something unsavory.

On the third set of knocks, I walked toward the door. I had to overcome the fear I felt, both of my feelings for Mick and what finding out the truth would do to our potential relationship. I had to put the story first.

As I pulled open the door, Mick pushed his way inside with two bags of groceries.

"A moment longer and I'm sure I would have been caught in your dorm!" He frowned as he set the bags down on the counter, then turned to look at me. "Didn't you hear me knocking?"

"I'm sorry." I brushed my wet hair back over my shoulders. "I was in the shower." The moment I said those words, I regretted them. I knew what I'd thought about when he'd mentioned that he needed a shower, and as I met his eyes, I sensed that he was thinking something quite similar about me.

I blushed as I lowered my eyes. "I didn't think you'd really be able to sneak in."

"You should never doubt me." He smiled as he walked over to me. "If I say I'm going to do something, I always find a way to do it." He wrapped his arms around my waist and looked into my eyes. "I am going to cook you something delicious, I promise."

"That's sweet." I forced myself to smile in return. If he sensed that something had changed between us, he might walk away from me before I had the chance to ask the questions that I needed to ask. "How can I help?" I pulled away from him and walked in the direction of the kitchen. "Let me get this stuff out for you."

"No way." He caught me around the waist and pulled me back away from the kitchen. "You have one job." He released me and grabbed my hand instead, then led me toward the sofa. "It's to relax." He gave me a light push down onto the soft cushions. Then he grabbed the remote on the table beside the sofa and turned on some music. "Should we light some of these candles?"

"No!" I spat the word out as my heart pounded.

"No?" He laughed. "Why not?"

"Oh, um, fire." I shrugged. "I'm not that fond of it. I mean, candles are pretty dangerous."

"I guess." He quirked an eyebrow then nodded. "Alright, no candles. Dinner won't take me long." He walked back into the kitchen.

I breathed a sigh of relief for the distance between us, however much the memory of his touch lingered and left sparks of pleasure behind. My mind swam as I tried to remember the things I wanted to ask him.

"I noticed that Ty wasn't part of the game yesterday. I heard he's a pretty good player." I glanced over my shoulder at Mick as he prepared the food he'd brought.

"He's a great player—one of the best I've ever seen." He grabbed two plates from the cabinet.

"So, why wasn't he in the game?"

"I don't know. Coach just doesn't play him."

Lie. "Oh. That seems strange. I would think he would want to play someone as talented as Ty."

"What's all this about Ty?" He flashed me a smile. "Do I need to worry about him? Is it all that blond hair? It gets all the girls."

"No." I forced a laugh. "I was just curious."

"That's what I like about you." He began to chop up some vegetables. "You're so curious about everything."

"I am. You told me that your stepfather got you into this school. Does he come to see your games?"

"No." He scraped the vegetables onto our plates.

"Why not?" I stood up and walked toward the kitchen. I sensed that I'd touched on a topic that he wanted to avoid.

"He's a busy guy." He cleared his throat. "I brought us some tea. I hope you'll like it." He pulled out a bottle of tea.

"Thanks." I took the bottle, then walked over to the cabinet and pulled out two glasses. "I'm sorry he doesn't come to see you play. He's missing out. You're so talented." I drew a sharp breath when I felt his hands on my hips. His cheek brushed along the side of my head and his lips neared my cheek.

"You think so?"

"I do." I shivered as his voice curled around my senses and swallowed up any questions that floated through my mind.

"I play even better when I know you're watching." He turned me around to face him. "It's embarrassing, really—the way I try to show off."

"You don't have to do anything to impress me." I stared into his eyes, caught between him and the counter.

"I feel like I do." He brushed my hair away from my cheek.

"The way you look at me—it's like you're always searching for something."

"It's just my nature." I willed myself to look away from him, but I just couldn't. "I always want to know more."

"More about what?" His hand settled on my shoulder, while his other hand remained on my hip. "You can ask me anything."

"It seems like you're closer to Coach Baker than the other players. I thought maybe that was because your stepfather isn't around much." My heart slammed against my chest as I wondered how he would react to the question.

"I tell you that you can ask me about anything and that's what you want to know? About Coach Baker?" He smiled as he leaned closer to me. "Maybe it's him I need to worry about."

"Not at all." I winced at the thought.

"You don't like him much, do you?" He shook his head. "I can't quite figure you out, Lala. You fight your way onto the cheerleading squad, but you act like you're better than everyone else once you're on it. You write articles about the football team that aren't very flattering, then you talk about my skills. Sometimes I'm not sure whether you're being straight with me."

I took a sharp breath as I sensed how close he was to discovering the truth about me. I couldn't let that happen. I had to distract him before he was able to put two and two together.

"I can't help it if I have a crush on you." I smiled as I gazed back at him. "I find it to be pretty confusing myself. But every time I see you—on the field or off—you're all I can think about."

"Yeah?" He pulled me closer to him away from the counter. "You really think I'm going to believe that you have a crush on me?"

"I do." I whispered the words. I wanted them to be a lie, but I knew that they weren't. In that moment, as he leaned so close that we could easily kiss, I wanted more than anything to feel his lips against mine. I didn't care about any envelope full of cash or what might really be going on behind the scenes. I wanted him to kiss me and wash away everything that weighed on my mind.

"Well, just wait until you try my food." He murmured his words with a grin, then his lips brushed my cheek. "Then you're going to fall in love."

SEVENTEEN

My heart skipped a beat.

Mick cleared his throat and took a step away from me. "I'm sorry, that probably ruined the moment." He chuckled. "Maby always tells me that I move too fast."

"It's okay." I captured his hand with my own. "I don't mind."

"Good." He glanced back at me. "Now let's eat." He picked up the plates and carried them to the table.

I felt his absence like a wave retreating back to the ocean. It was as if my whole world receded for a moment and I forgot to even exist. As I picked up the glasses, my hands trembled. He thought I would fall in love over his food, but what if it was already too late? What if playing this game of wanting him had led me down a path I couldn't turn back from?

"You okay?" He met my eyes as I walked carefully to the table. "You are hungry, aren't you?"

"Starving."

"Good." He pulled out my chair for me as I set down the glasses.

With every breath I took, I found myself a little more lost.

The conflict of whether I could continue to hide my intentions was drowned out by the insistent pounding of my heart. I settled in my chair, then looked across the table at him as he sat down as well.

"Thanks for doing this, Mick, it's sweet."

"After seeing how hard you worked out there today, I knew you'd be pretty wiped out. That food in the cafeteria isn't enough to keep you in shape when you're working out like that." He picked up his glass and took a sip. "Plus, it's a great excuse to get you alone."

I smiled to myself. While some guys might encourage me to slim down, it seemed as if Mick liked my curves. Just another reason to find him endearing.

"You don't need an excuse to get me alone." I met his eyes. "I enjoy my time with you."

"I appreciate that." He picked up his fork and pushed some of his food around on his plate, then looked up at me again. "So why does it feel like you're holding back?"

"I'm not."

"I don't believe you." He smirked. "I think you're lying to me."

My eyes widened as I looked at him. Could he really read me that well?

"But that's okay." He sat back in his chair. "If you need time to open up, I understand. Just because I feel comfortable with you, that doesn't mean that you feel the same with me."

"I just have some things on my mind." I took a bite of my food and hoped that would be enough to satisfy him.

"I'm here to listen. Anytime you need to talk."

"Thanks." I held back a rush of desire. How could he say all the right things? How could he be just so perfect and absolutely not perfect at the same time?

"I'm sure you have some things that you're keeping from me

too." I met his eyes as I spoke. "Things that you're not ready to share with me."

"I'm an open book." He grinned. "Nothing to hide."

Another lie. My stomach twisted. If he could lie to my face that easily, then yes, I was the fool that was being conned, not the other way around.

"Nothing?" I raised an eyebrow as I took another bite of my food.

"Well, there are some things in my life that are difficult." He drew a slow breath, then shook his head. "But that's not something I want to talk about now. Not when there are so many good things to discuss. Like how amazing it is to be here, sitting across from you."

"I'm enjoying this too." I leaned forward some. "But don't make it seem like I'm the only one holding back. I know something is bothering you. I can see it."

"You can?" His eyes widened. "What do you see?"

"I don't know exactly. But I know it's there."

"That's that curious mind of yours." He smiled. "I can see you digging, always digging."

"What am I going to find?" I took another bite of my food. "Something I like? Something I don't?"

"I guess that depends." He looked down at his plate.

"Depends on what?"

"On how much you like me." He smiled as he looked up again. "On how much you're willing to forgive?"

Those words struck me hard as he stared at me. How much was I willing to forgive? I enjoyed sitting across from him. I enjoyed his eyes on mine. I enjoyed his hand as it glided across mine and the flutter in my chest as he curled his fingers around mine. I enjoyed the way he looked at me with such admiration and desire. How could I not?

My cheeks flushed.

I closed my eyes briefly, then focused on the memory of that morning. Yes, something underhanded was going on. There was no question of that. But so what?

I opened my eyes again and looked at him.

"Mick, I think you're a good person." I felt the honesty that rippled through my words. I did think he was a good person. That didn't mean that he made good choices. "And I don't think anything could change that."

I forced myself not to wince at the lie. I was worried. I was worried that I would find out the truth about his involvement with Coach Baker, and all the crazy emotions I'd experienced since the day he'd caught me falling off the bleachers would have been for nothing. How much could I forgive? How much was I willing to overlook?

If I went by the ache in the pit of my stomach as he smiled at me, I'd believe that I could forgive absolutely anything as long as it meant he continued to hold my hand.

But I couldn't just go by that. It was more than just my desire for him. It was more than just the heart that pounded against my chest when he leaned across the table to whisper to me.

"Lala, you see me in a way that I don't think anyone ever has."

There it was, the truth. It settled between us like an uninvited guest. In his mind, it meant I knew him better than anyone else. But in my mind, it meant that I knew his secrets. Secrets that were destined to keep us apart.

I steered the topic of conversation back toward football and he eagerly discussed some of his favorite plays and players. I pretended to be interested, and instead, just felt relief that the heavy questions could be avoided for a few minutes. Maybe I wanted to pretend that we were just two students sharing a meal.

"Let me clean this up." I started to pick up our empty plates.

"Not a chance." He waved me away. "I'm full service." He grinned as he carried the plates and glasses to the sink. "Did you enjoy it?" He looked at me as he began to wash the dishes.

"Absolutely. Your mother did teach you well. Do you miss her?" I leaned against the other side of the counter.

"I do. We talk now and then, but she's been busy lately. Working a lot."

"What does she do?"

"Whatever work she can find." He shrugged. "Mostly retail."

"Really?" I narrowed my eyes. "Does she just like to keep busy? It seems like she wouldn't have to work if she didn't want to."

He dropped one of the plates onto the counter as he set it aside. "Oops." He frowned as he checked to make sure it wasn't cracked. "Sorry, I got distracted."

"Don't worry about it." I met his eyes and noticed some strain there. Was he hiding something again?

"Why don't we watch a movie?" He walked around the counter toward the sofa. "Anything you're interested in seeing?"

"I'll let you pick." I followed him to the sofa. I noticed that he didn't answer my question but decided not to press it. As I settled beside him, he wrapped his arm around my shoulders and pulled me close.

"Thanks for a wonderful evening, Lala."

"You're the one who made it wonderful." I tipped my head against his shoulder.

The movie started. I wished with all of my strength that just for that moment, we could be any normal couple, snuggling on the sofa together for the first time.

Instead, my mind wandered.

What about that envelope, Mick?

EIGHTEEN

About halfway through the movie, I couldn't stand it anymore. Mick's arm around me and his scent surrounding me made me think all kinds of ridiculous things. I needed to get away from him before I lost all control of my mind.

"Mick, this was great, but I'm feeling kind of tired." I slipped out from under his arm and stood up.

"The movie isn't over." He glanced over at me—obviously confused—and stood up as well.

"I know, I'm sorry. You were right, I really overdid it out there today. I'm a little too sore for sitting on the sofa and I think I need to just rest a little." I turned to face him. "I'm so sorry. I hope you don't mind that I'm flaking out on you."

"I don't mind." He met my eyes as he crossed the distance between us. "Why don't you let me work on your shoulders a bit?" He ran his hands along the tops of them.

"It's okay." I started to step back.

"Don't worry." He smiled. "I do this for the guys on the team. I promise, I'll behave."

"Mick, really, I just think I need to lie down."

"And I'll let you, after you let me work my magic fingers."

He guided me down into a chair. "Just try to relax. If it doesn't feel amazing, I'll stop."

I didn't know how to deny him. The truth was, my shoulders did ache.

As he began to rub them, I felt warmth flow through my skin. It eased the pain that traveled through them almost instantly.

"Wow."

"I know." He laughed. "That's what everyone says. Just lean back, I'll take care of you." He brushed my hair away from my shoulders, then continued the massage.

It did feel good. My muscles relaxed. But then it became something more.

My skin tingled where he touched it. My breath was laced with the scent of his cologne as he leaned over me. I wanted more than just his hands on my shoulders. I wanted his arms around me again. I wanted to forget all the reasons why I should resist.

What if I did? What if I did just forget?

I closed my eyes as he continued, his hands moving a little ways down my shoulders and onto my arms. His fingertips glided against my bare skin and my heartbeat quickened. What if I just let myself feel this instead of trying to control it? My whole world could change. I could be swept up in something I never thought I'd experience, something more wonderful than I'd ever imagined.

"Lala, I'd better stop." He breathed his words and only then did I realize that his cheek hovered right beside mine, his hands had reached my forearms and his fingers stroked down along my wrists, which rested against my thighs. I felt a shiver in his touch as he trailed his hands up along my arms again.

"You don't have to." I tilted my head back as I looked up at him.

He stood over me, his eyes charged with heat and his lips parted in a way that made me wonder what it would be like to kiss him.

"I do." He took a slow breath. "I promised you I would behave, and right now, that's the last thing I want to do."

"Mick." I stood up from the chair and turned to face him. "I've never felt like this with anyone before."

"Neither have I."

I searched his expression for any hint of deceit. How was it possible that a popular boy like him—the star of the football team, sought after by just about every girl at Oak Brook Academy—could feel differently about me? But he gazed at me with such openness, I couldn't doubt him.

"I want to see where this goes." My heart skipped a beat as I spoke those words. It wasn't just to draw him in so that I could learn more about the team or Coach Baker. I meant them. At that point, I couldn't imagine walking away from him and whatever it was that crackled between us.

He wrapped his arm around my shoulders and it felt as if every nerve in my body came alive. He leaned his face toward mine and I ached to crush my lips against his.

"So do I, Lala, more than anything." He searched my eyes. "Meet me tomorrow. At the secret place. Before the sun comes up. Will you be there?"

"I'll be there." My heart pounded. I wanted to cup his cheeks and steer his lips to mine, but he pulled away before I could.

"Until then, my acrobat. Get some rest." He caught my hand, gave it a light squeeze, then headed for the door.

I thought about following him out. I thought about demanding the kiss that I wanted so badly.

But I didn't. I let the door shut behind him. I let my body

collapse back down on the sofa. I closed my eyes and waited for the dizziness in my mind to pass.

What kind of spell did he cast over me that I couldn't even think straight? I'd never believed my friends when they claimed to feel so strongly for a boy. It was silly. We were too young to feel something so strong.

But Mick had changed all that for me. Just by being who he was. How could I stop myself from going after him when every muscle in my body ached for him?

I trailed my fingertips along my wrist where he'd last massaged and wondered if I could still feel the warmth of his touch. Maybe it was wrong. Maybe he was caught up in something that he shouldn't have been. But I didn't care anymore. All I cared about was being with him.

That night I could barely sleep as I thought about meeting him. Why did he want to meet me so early? Why at the secret place? Would I be able to get outside before we were technically allowed to leave the dorm?

When my alarm went off the next morning, all of these thoughts continued to race through my mind. I dressed for the day, threw my hair back into a loose ponytail, then crept through the dorm room.

Cyndi had come home at some point. I'd heard her door. But now the dorm was quiet. Not just our room, but the entire dorm.

I'd never tried to sneak out before. I broke out into a sweat just thinking about it. What if I was caught? I pushed the thought from my mind. No matter what, I had to get to Mick. If it meant risking a detention or worse, I was okay with that.

I stepped out of the dorm and into the hall. Again, perfectly quiet.

Outside it was still dark, with just hints of the sun beginning to color the sky. Would Mick be there when I arrived?

I held my breath as I hurried through the courtyard. I knew security guards patrolled the grounds at night. Would they still be out?

I ran past the library with my heart in my throat.

By the time I made it to the old building, my heart was racing. There, against the dark sky, I could see a shadow moving on the roof.

"Lala!" He called to me in a loud whisper. "Hurry, come on up."

I stared for a moment. In that moment, I was me again—me before Mick. I was the me that would question why I would want to go on the roof of an essentially abandoned building, why I would risk breaking many rules just for a boy's company.

But that moment passed with the next slam of my heartbeat and I headed into the building. I ran up the stairs and out onto the roof.

As I stepped through the door, Mick turned to face me. The wind teased his hair, the last traces of moonlight giving his skin a silvery glow. He wasn't just some boy. He was the most handsome guy I'd ever laid eyes on and he walked straight toward me with his hand outstretched.

My knees trembled. My breath caught in my throat. All that mattered was the warmth of his hand as it curled around mine and the way he looked at me, as if I was the most beautiful being he'd ever seen.

NINETEEN

"Alana, you're so beautiful." He pulled me into his arms against his chest.

I rested my head briefly against his shoulder as I felt his chest rise with every breath he took.

In the chill of the morning air, he tightened his arms around me. I let my head settle on his shoulder again. I wanted that moment to last an eternity. Nothing needed to be said, nothing needed to be explained. I just wanted to savor his warmth, the sound of his breath as it trailed along the skin of my cheek, and the touch of his fingers that stroked through my hair.

My heart slammed against my chest as I fought the drive to tip my head up toward him and meet his lips with mine. I wanted to be in control, but at the same time, I didn't. I wanted to be able to let go, to be as free as the wind that blew lightly across the roof.

Maybe it didn't have to matter that he was involved in anything. Maybe I didn't have to care.

"Lala," he whispered as his palm cupped my chin.

I looked up at him in the same moment that he looked down at me, and our lips collided. To say who kissed whom would be impossible. It was as if in the same instant neither of us could continue to resist.

The sweet soft kiss barely lasted a few seconds before Mick pulled back and looked into my eyes.

"No matter what we face, I think we can handle it if we're together."

"Me too." I pulled him back toward me for another kiss.

As I lost myself in it, his arms wrapped around me and the world around us began to light up. Even as the sun climbed higher in the sky, I continued to kiss him. Logically, I knew that our magical moment had to come to an end, but I pushed the thought away. I wanted it to last as long as it possibly could.

Mick pulled away again, this time breathless, as he looked at me. "I'm sorry."

"You have nothing to be sorry for." I smiled as I met his eyes.

"I'm sorry because we have to go." He clasped my hands with his own. "It's daylight now and the security guard will be riding through here. If he spots us, he'll figure out that we've been using this place as a hideout. We can't let that happen."

"No, we can't." My heart dropped at the thought.

"I wish we could stay here forever." He inched close to me and met my lips again.

I pressed my hand against his chest as I returned the kiss, then reluctantly broke it.

"You're right, we have to go." I touched his cheek and smiled as I studied the glow in his eyes.

"But I don't want to walk away from you."

"You don't have to." I squeezed the hand I still held. "Mick, we might have to be apart for a little while, but not for long."

"I'll see you at lunch?" He leaned close, as if he might kiss me again, but ducked away as we both heard an engine in the distance.

"Lunch." I nodded. "We need to get out of here."

"You first." He pointed to the door that led to the roof. "I'll make sure no one spots you."

"My hero." I winked at him as I hurried toward the door.

I wanted to say a lot more than that. I wanted to tell him how I really felt—that I wanted to spend every moment with him. But with each step I descended, I felt the real world reaching out for me.

Up on that roof, with his arms around me, everything was different. It was like living in a fantasy, but the moment I stepped out of that building, life hit me. A life that included my work as an investigative reporter. A life that Coach Baker existed in and that Hallie had disappeared from. I couldn't just pretend that these things weren't happening, could I?

I hurried toward the dormitory to collect my things for class. I still needed to find a way to make it all work. But I was determined that I could. As I stepped into my dorm room, Cyndi greeted me with a glare.

"And just where were you? I was going to wake you up for school five minutes ago, and when you weren't in there, I freaked out!"

"Oh no, you didn't call anyone, did you?" My eyes widened at the thought.

"No, I figured you were out sneaking around somewhere." She wiggled her eyebrows. "With Mick?"

"Maybe." I grinned as I walked past her toward my room.

"I knew it!" She clapped her hands together. "I have to say that I never expected you and Mick to hit it off. But if it works, it works!"

It doesn't. I closed my eyes briefly to try to block out that thought. I grabbed my backpack and shoved in the books and homework that I needed. I did my best to ignore the pile of research on my desk. The article would have to wait. At least for the moment. At least until I could figure a few things out.

"He's a pretty amazing person." I paused in front of Cyndi and smiled.

"Did you kiss?" Cyndi stared straight into my eyes. "You did, didn't you?" She squealed. "I can see it in your face! You're glowing!"

"I am not!" I rolled my eyes, then laughed. Her excitement stirred mine.

"How was it?" She flopped back against the sofa and pressed her hands against her chest. "Was it like, 'Oops, I tripped and fell and my lips just happened to land on yours'? Or was it more like, 'Oh darling, I've been waiting for this moment for centuries'!"

"I haven't been alive for centuries." I grinned.

"You have to tell me!" She jumped up and frowned.

"I have to get to class." I waved to her as I hurried out the door. "I promise, more details later!"

"Details?" Maby crossed my path in the hallway outside of my dorm room. "Details about what?" She linked her arm with mine as we continued toward the common room.

"Nothing." I grinned.

"Oh, oh, I know that look!" She squeezed my arm. "Is it official?"

"Official?" I blinked.

"I mean, boyfriend and girlfriend official. Are you and Mick a thing now?"

Her question hung in the air around me. I had no idea how to answer it. Mick and I hadn't actually talked about anything. All we'd done was kiss.

Had it been just a kiss? Maybe he didn't want anything more than that. Maybe now that he'd had that first kiss, he'd decide that there were other girls he liked better.

My stomach churned at the thought.

"Uh no, nothing is official." I pushed through the door of the common room out into the courtyard. "I'll catch up with you later, Maby, I have to get to class!" I broke into a jog across the courtyard. I needed to create some distance and give myself some chance to sort things out in my mind.

I was almost to my class when I spotted Mr. Raynaud outside in the hall. He met my eyes as I approached.

"Alana, I haven't seen much of you lately." He raised an eyebrow. "I hope you weren't upset about my rejecting your story proposal."

"No, I'm fine, I understand." My heart pounded as I looked into his eyes. "Just busy."

"I hear you've joined the cheerleading squad." He crossed his arms. "That won't leave you much time for the newspaper."

"I promise it won't interfere."

"I hope not. You're quite talented, Alana, I hope you know that. The new issue is due to come out on Monday. I hope that you'll have something for me before then." He glanced at his watch, then looked up at me. "Can I expect an article from you?"

"Yes, of course. I'll have it for you soon." I forced a smile.

"Good." He nodded to me, then continued down the hall.

It warmed my heart to know that he thought I was talented, but I guessed that his tune would change when the truth came out. I didn't have any other article for him—only the one that threatened to expose Coach Baker and possibly end my attendance at Oak Brook Academy.

Throughout the morning, my mind shifted from the elation of my first kiss with Mick to the pressure of whether to continue researching the article. I knew that if I continued, I'd likely stumble over something I couldn't unsee, something that might change how I felt about Mick.

But could I live with myself if I let the story go?

TWENTY

When the bell rang for lunch, I was still conflicted. I knew that Mick would be waiting for me in the cafeteria. But how could I look him in the eye when I hadn't made a decision yet?

I thought that I could forget about the article, but the more I tried, the more it nagged at me. Hallie had lost her position on the cheerleading squad because of me. Could I just ignore that? It wasn't fair. None of it was fair. Someone had to do something about it. Until Mick, I'd been determined that the someone would be me. Now, I wasn't sure what to do, but I knew that I couldn't see him.

Instead of going in the direction of the cafeteria, I headed for the library. Not many people opted to spend the lunch hour there. The few who did, I didn't know very well. I was glad that they seemed content to keep to themselves, while I settled at one of the tables and pulled out my notebook.

I read over the log of evidence that I'd been keeping. Each piece awakened my desire to get to the truth. Coach Baker shouldn't be allowed to get away with whatever it was he was doing. I was the only one that had any interest in stopping him.

When a chair was pulled up next to mine, I looked up to see Hallie.

"Hallie." I met her eyes. "I'm so sorry."

"Don't be." She forced a smile. "It's not your fault. I knew the consequences I would face when I took your side."

"But you shouldn't have to face them." I frowned as I studied her. "Can't you take it to the principal and demand to be reinstated?"

"Not a chance. Everything goes through Coach Baker since he's the head of the athletics department, and he doesn't let complaints about the athletes or the cheerleaders get further than him. There's no point." She shrugged. "There's nothing anybody can do."

"What if you tell her that you were wrong? You don't have to take my side. You can take Sherry's instead."

"No, I couldn't." She took a deep breath. "I can't go against what I believe in. Besides, you're the best thing that has happened to the cheerleading squad. You have more skills than anyone else on the team. Whether Sherry wants to admit it or not, she needs you."

"This just isn't right."

"You're right, it isn't. But that's just how things work here at Oak Brook Academy. Anyway, I just wanted to warn you about something." She leaned closer to me. "The night of the party, when Mick pushed you in the pool..."

"Yes?" I narrowed my eyes.

"Sherry knows that Graham gave you a ride back to the dorm. I'd be very careful if I were you. She doesn't like to share."

"Share?" I winced. "It was just a ride."

"Maybe it was. But Sherry won't see it that way." She gave my hand a light pat. "Good luck, Alana—with everything." She stood up and walked away.

I thought about going after her, but what could I say? Could I promise her that I would change everything? That I would expose the truth? Could I sacrifice any chance I had with Mick in the process?

As the afternoon crept by, I thought about seeing Mick during practice. He would already be annoyed that I hadn't shown up for lunch. I knew he would want to speak to me. But how could I be face to face with him?

Luckily, before the final bell sounded, rain began to pour down outside. The afternoon athletics activities would be canceled. I breathed a sigh of relief, but I knew that it wouldn't last long. I couldn't go back to my dorm; Mick would find me there. Instead, I decided to go to the one person whose advice I thought I could trust.

I knocked on Maby's door and waited for her to answer.

"Lala." Maby grinned as she held the door open for me. "I thought I might get a visit from you."

"You did?" I stepped inside.

"Well, considering that Mick has been raving about you all day, my guess is that things have gotten more serious between you two."

"Maby, I just don't know." I took a deep breath as I sprawled out across her sofa. "Nothing like this has ever happened to me before. I don't know how to make sense of it."

"Well I can tell you to give up on that now." Maby laughed as she picked up my feet, then sat down on the sofa beside me. She dropped my feet down in her lap. "From what I hear, once you're head over heels, you can't find your way back."

"From what you hear?" I looked up at her. "Are you saying you've never felt that way?"

"Never. But that's on purpose. I have no interest in anything like that while I'm in high school. To me that's just a waste of time and energy. All I want to do is enjoy my freedom while I can."

I thought about the security guard that had interrupted my special moment with Mick. I thought about Coach Baker and the way that he seemed to have control over Mick.

"Do you really feel free here?"

"It may not be perfect, but it works for me." She patted one of my feet. "None of that matters. What matters is that you're happy and so is Mick. That's what you should be thinking about."

"I am thinking about it. That's the problem." I rolled my eyes. "It feels like the only thing that I can think about. I feel kind of ridiculous."

"Oh, it's just new." She shrugged. "Why not enjoy it?"

"Because." I bit back my next words. I couldn't tell Maby about Coach Baker or what I suspected was happening between him and Mick. I couldn't explain that even though I was very happy to be involved with Mick at this point, the memory of that meeting between them still weighed on my mind in a way that I couldn't ignore.

"Because why?" She laughed. "A sweet, beautiful guy adores you. What could be wrong with that?"

What could be wrong with that? I repeated the question in my mind.

"Nothing. Nothing at all. You're right." I stood up from the sofa. "Thanks, Maby."

"Lala, what's wrong?" Maby stood up as well.

"Nothing." I smiled. "Thanks for your advice."

"I know it's not nothing." She frowned as she looked into my eyes. "Something is weighing on that mind."

"It looks like the rain has stopped. I'm going to go for a walk." I gave her a quick wave, then headed out the door. If I'd stayed a moment longer, I might have told her everything. But wouldn't she be angry with me? Wouldn't she be upset that I had used Mick to get information?

I was sure that Mick would be if he ever found out.

My mind swirled as I headed out of the dormitory and into the courtyard. I needed more time to think things through.

My phone rang. I checked it and saw Mick's name on the screen.

Of course he'd call. I'd been avoiding him all day.

I sent the call to voicemail. Seconds later, I received a text.

LALA, are you okay? Was this morning too fast? You can tell me. Just let me know what's going on.

MY HEART ACHED at the thought of his being upset and worried. I'd gone from the euphoria of the kiss we'd shared to absolute confusion. If I didn't pursue the article, people would continue to be treated unfairly. Coach Baker would get away with everything.

Anger rocketed through me. Could I let that happen?

But if I told the truth, if I continued to dig deeper, then not only was Mick's future at risk, our relationship was sure to fall apart before it even had the chance to get started. I never thought he would be a problem. I never imagined I could feel this way about anyone. Now that I did, I understood what all the poetry and heartbreaking songs were about. I understood that sometimes love could turn your world completely upside down.

My fingers trembled as I typed back a quick response.

. . .

I'M FINE. Talk later.

AS I HIT SEND, I wondered if that would be true. I had to make a decision and I had to make it soon.

TWENTY-ONE

As the evening progressed, I walked along the football field. The scent of damp grass and fresh air filled my nose. I would have found it beautiful if I weren't so distracted by thoughts of Mick.

It had been hard not to see him that afternoon. I could have hunted him down, but instead I'd gone to Maby. I wasn't quite sure why. I knew that I trusted her because she was the most honest person I knew. Perhaps I hoped that she would talk some sense into me. Instead, she'd encouraged me to continue things with Mick.

As I rounded the corner of the field, I noticed someone else strolling alone. Coach Baker. He had his phone pressed to his ear as he moved quickly back toward the school.

My investigative instincts kicked in. I needed to find out what he was up to, and listening in on a phone conversation could definitely help with that. As I drew closer to him, I heard his voice rise.

"No, that's not an option. You need to listen to me."

My chest tightened at the tone he used. He sounded less like a football coach and more like a mob boss.

"I don't care what you think. I'm not sure why you think I

should. I've told you what I expect you to do. I won't tolerate anything less."

As he paused, I realized that all he had to do was turn around. Then he would know that I was following him. What would he do if he caught me?

I decided not to give him the chance and started to walk off across the field. But as I did, I caught the last snippet of his conversation.

"Mick, don't test me. I've warned you about this. This is your last chance." He hung up the phone.

His words struck me hard. Mick. Yes, of course he was talking to Mick. Why wouldn't he be? It was Mick that had given him an envelope full of money, wasn't it? It was Mick that I tried to pretend wasn't involved in all of this.

The reminder made my head spin.

A quick glance over my shoulder revealed that Coach Baker had walked off in the other direction. If he'd noticed me, he didn't show any sign of it.

I was safe. But that didn't matter much to the ache in my stomach.

Yes, I wanted to be with Mick, but how long could I actually ignore his involvement? How much was I willing to sacrifice in order to continue to pretend that Mick and I could be together?

By the time I returned to my dorm room, I knew what I had to do. I had to get to the truth and that included finding out exactly how Mick was involved with Coach Baker. I couldn't be in the dark any longer, even if it meant that any chance that Mick and I had of being together would be ruined.

I sat down with my computer and I began to dig into Mick. It was pretty easy to find information about him at the school. He was in just about every picture on the school's website. He and his football buddies popped up at just about every event that the school held.

I noticed as I looked through the pictures that Ty appeared by his side in most of them. It was clear that the two were closer friends that I had first assumed. Mick had stood up to Coach Baker for Ty's sake. He obviously thought his friend wasn't being treated fairly. Maybe Ty was the key to finding out more about Mick's involvement.

I closed my computer, then jumped as I heard a knock on the dorm room door. Would it be Mick outside? Would he demand to know why I'd been avoiding him? He hadn't texted me again since I'd texted him back. Maybe he had decided to just show up at my door. He'd made it clear that the rules didn't apply to him, that he always found a way around them.

I took a deep breath as I walked over to the door and braced myself for whoever might be on the other side.

When I opened it, I was surprised to find Fi.

"Hey, Lala, thought I'd check on you." She pushed her way into the dorm room.

"Why?" I turned to face her.

"Maby told me about you and Mick." She dropped down on the sofa and looked up at me. "It's rough, isn't it?"

"That Maby told you my personal business?" I crossed my arms.

"Oh, once you're part of our little group, there aren't any secrets." Fi smiled. "It's part of the charm."

"Is it?" I raised an eyebrow. "It seems a little intrusive to me."

"Trust me, you'll grow to love it." She grinned. "Anyway, I thought you might want to talk." She patted the sofa beside her. "Was I wrong?"

"Not exactly." I sat down and looked over at her. "Honestly, I'm not sure what I can say."

"You don't have to give me all the details—unless you want to." She shrugged. "I know what it's like to fall in love with someone you didn't expect to even like. It's a battle. It's confusing."

"Yes, it's definitely all those things." I closed my eyes. "I just wish that I could figure it all out. I wish it would make sense."

"It does make sense."

"It does?" I opened my eyes and looked at her.

"It does if you let it. As long as you try to fight it, as long as you try to run from it—it's not going to make sense. But the moment that you let it happen, it will all make perfect sense." She smiled. "I'm not telling you what to do, Lala—that's up to you. But I'm telling you that it's not as complicated as it seems. It's only complicated because you think you're still in control."

"I am in control." I stood up from the sofa.

"No, you *want* to be in control." She stood up as well. "But that doesn't mean that you are. Right now, your emotions are in charge—whether you like it or not—and they are going to stay in charge until you make some choices."

"That's what I'm trying to do." I began to pace back and forth across the living room.

"No, you're not. You think you are. But what you're trying to do is make a choice on the surface. You're going to decide what you think is best and do that, but underneath you're still going to want something else, which means you haven't actually made the choice."

"Ugh, see, it is complicated!" I laughed as I rolled my eyes.

"It's not, unless you make it that way. If you make the choice you actually want, then there's nothing complicated about it." She stood up from the sofa and walked over to me. "Look, I know it's overwhelming. I think Mick is a pretty good guy. But that doesn't make me right. And it doesn't mean that you should take my word for it. I think you're a pretty interesting person. But I don't know you very well. I'm someone looking from the outside in, and I'm only here because I know what it's like to feel torn in different directions." She took my hand as she looked into my eyes. "Don't torture yourself. You have to make the choice that you can live with. That's the best advice I can offer."

"Did it work for you?"

"It did." She smiled. "I've never been happier." She shrugged. "I just had to get out of my own way."

As Fi left my dorm room, I thought about what she had to say.

What was the choice I could live with? Could I really embrace my feelings for Mick and forget all about the article I wanted to write?

I thought about Hallie and the position she'd lost on the squad. I thought about Ty and the bench he seemed to be banished to.

Maybe it wasn't even about me.

I couldn't make a clear choice, not without knowing more anyway.

TWENTY-TWO

Hunting down Ty was not as easy as I'd anticipated. Everywhere I went and asked about him, I was told that he'd just left. He wasn't in the courtyard or the cafeteria.

As it neared dinner time, I felt the pressure of knowing that I couldn't avoid Mick forever. He was eventually going to catch up to me and want to know what was going on. I couldn't blame him. If it was him treating me this way after the amazing kiss we'd shared, I'd be certain that he didn't care about me at all.

That wasn't the case. In fact, the problem was that I cared far too much. I wanted to protect him, to somehow shield him from whatever he was involved in. But I didn't even know if that was possible.

With my focus on Ty, I could at least take a break from thinking about Mick.

I was about to give up and head to the cafeteria, when I heard the grind of wheels against pavement right behind me.

Ty skidded to a stop on his skateboard, then met my eyes.

"I hear you've been looking for me."

"I have been." I watched as he pushed his long blond hair away from his eyes.

"Why?" He stared at me.

"I have some questions for you."

"About what?" He tilted his head to the side. "I don't think I even know you."

"You don't."

"You're that new cheerleader, aren't you?" He smiled some. "Mick's girl."

Mick's girl. The words echoed through my mind and caused a surprising spark within me. I didn't think I'd ever like being called anyone's girl, but with Mick, it felt a little different.

"I don't know about that. But we're friends."

"Friends." He nodded. "Okay. So, what do you want to ask me?"

"I've noticed you don't play." I looked toward the football field. "You just sit on the bench during the games."

"So?" He grinned. "I'm not the best."

"That's not what Mick says."

"Oh?" He cleared his throat. "Well, Mick's a good friend."

"You started here this year, right?" I noticed that his school uniform was a little faded and worn along the creases. I had five of my own and replaced them at the first sign of wear.

"Yes. On scholarship." His cheeks flushed.

"I think that's great. What did you get the scholarship for?"

"What's with all the questions?" He crossed his arms. "I'm not sure I want to answer. Aren't you some kind of reporter?"

"I work at the school newspaper, yes." I stared at him. "I'm just curious, Ty. I heard that you got the scholarship because you were such a good football player. Now you're sitting on the bench."

"Yeah, well, I guess I'm not as good as the rest of them."

"That's not what Mick says." I locked my eyes to his.

"Mick doesn't know what he's talking about." He stuck one

foot on his skateboard and began to rock it back and forth. "And if you were smart, you'd stop asking so many questions."

"All I want to know is, why aren't you complaining to someone about being stuck on the bench?"

"When you're given a hand-out, you don't complain." He snapped his words, then pushed off the ground with one foot.

As he sailed past me on his skateboard, I did my best to hold in my frustration. If I thought I was going to get anything useful out of him, I was wrong.

I turned back toward the cafeteria just in time to see Mick headed in my direction. There was no avoiding him now. No excuse to escape him. Still, I wasn't ready to see him.

I turned and started in the other direction.

"Don't walk away from me."

Mick jogged after me. I could hear him just behind me.

My chest tightened with a mixture of fear and dread. Would he be angry? Would he tell me that he wanted nothing to do with me?

"Lala, please. I've been so worried about you." He caught me by the shoulder.

"Worried?" I turned around to face him.

"You've been acting strange all day." He met my eyes. "You won't answer my calls!"

"I'm sorry Mick, I've just been busy." I looked down at my shoes.

"No, don't do that." He frowned as he stepped closer to me. "If you don't want to be around me, you can tell me that, but please, don't lie to me."

"Mick." I sighed as I felt the back of his hand brush along my cheek. "I'm sorry."

"For what?" He cupped my chin and guided my face up so that he could look into my eyes.

"Yeah, for what?" Sherry's voice cut through my thoughts. "Why don't you tell him, Alana? Or would you like me to?"

"Sherry." I glared at her as I took a step back from Mick.

"Leave us alone." Mick frowned as he wrapped his arm around my shoulder.

"Oh no, Mick, this concerns you too. I think you'd like to know about it." She smiled as she looked at him. "You see, maybe Alana is giving you the cold shoulder because you're not the football star she's looking to hook up with. You're not Graham." She looked back at me. "Isn't that right, Alana?"

"No, it's not." I glanced at Mick. "It has nothing to do with Graham."

"Graham?" Mick's eyes widened. "What are you talking about, Sherry?"

"She's lying, Mick." My heartbeat quickened as I recalled Hallie's warning. Had Sherry just been waiting for the right moment to try to drive a wedge between us?

"I'm lying, am I? So it wasn't you that spent the evening after the party with my boyfriend?" Sherry crossed the distance between us. "I know Graham can't be trusted, but really, Alana, you should know better."

"What is she talking about?" Mick's voice rose. "Are you into Graham? Is that what's happening here?"

"No!" I turned my attention back to Mick. His usually warm, brown eyes were cold and hard as he stared at me.

"So you weren't with him?"

"He gave me a ride home after the party." I crossed my arms. "That's all it was."

"Sure. You were alone in a car with Graham and nothing else happened." Sherry rolled her eyes. "Please don't try to act like I don't know Graham. I know him too well to think that he kept his hands off you." She smirked. "But I guess you're used to lying. I mean, you seem to be very good at it. Isn't she, Mick?"

"Mick, I'm not lying." I turned to face him and placed my hands on his chest.

"No? How would I know? You've been avoiding me all day and you won't tell me why." He caught my hands and held them against his chest. "I know Graham pretty well too. He doesn't just do favors for people. If something happened, you should just tell me now."

"Nothing happened, Mick." I stared hard into his eyes. "He just gave me a ride home."

"That doesn't sound like Graham to me."

"So you're going to trust Sherry over me?" Anger bubbled up within me. If things were going to end with Mick, it would be because of me, not because of some lie that Sherry told. "You know she has it in for me. You can't possibly believe her."

"I don't know what to believe." He squeezed my hands, then sighed. "One minute I think I have you figured out, the next you completely change. I know something is going on with you and I know you won't tell me what it is."

"She's playing both of you." Sherry shook her head. "She's just trying to string you along until Graham pays her enough attention. I mean, why would she want you, if she could have him?" Sherry fluffed her hair over her shoulder, then turned and walked away. "Too bad he's already taken!"

"What a piece of work!" I glared at Sherry, then looked back at Mick. "She's lying through her teeth."

"She's not the only one, is she?" He pulled me closer to him as he searched my eyes. "You never told me you were in Graham's car."

"Mick?" I stared at him. "You don't believe her, do you?"

"Like I said, I don't know what to believe. This morning, I thought we made it clear how we feel about each other, but now?" He shook his head. "I think you need to figure out what it is you want, because I'm not someone that likes to be played around with. If you're with me, you're not with anyone else, including Graham."

As he strode off, I thought about chasing after him. But my chest was too tight for me to even take a full breath.

If he couldn't believe me, then what was I trying to hold onto?

TWENTY-THREE

I stood frozen, left in the wake of Mick's anger and Sherry's chaos. As my heart pounded, I tried to make sense of what had just happened. My thoughts swirled through my mind no matter how hard I tried to pin them down. Mick thought I'd done something with Graham? I wanted to prove to him that nothing had happened, but that was impossible.

Instead, I could only start walking. I walked until I found myself outside the library. The only thing that made sense to me was getting to the truth. If Mick wanted to believe that I was interested in Graham, there wasn't much I could do about that. The only thing I did have some control over was finding out what was really happening in Mick's life. Maybe he didn't trust me, but I had good reason not to trust him.

As I stepped into the library, I tried to focus on the task at hand. I wanted to be able to turn my emotions off. Each time I started to shift my attention to something other than Mick, however, my heart began to race and instantly my thoughts returned to that moment when he'd walked away.

Was this really it? Did he want nothing to do with me now?

I hated the fact that it mattered to me so much and that it was a distraction.

Frustrated, I stood up suddenly from my chair and almost knocked it over as I did.

"Easy there." Graham caught the chair before it could topple over. "You don't want to upset the librarian. I think she's more strict than the principal."

"That might be true." I turned to face him. "We keep meeting here. Don't you have anything better to do than hang out in a library?" I sat down again, then scooted my chair closer to the table.

"Actually..." He smiled some. "I'll admit it, I came here because I thought you might be here. I heard about what happened earlier between you and Mick." He settled into the chair beside mine. "I'm sorry. That must have been rough."

"It was." I frowned as I stared hard at the notebook in front of me.

"Sherry can be so crazy." He groaned and leaned closer to me. "I'm sorry if she gave you a hard time."

"She seems to think that something happened between us that night that you gave me a ride home." I looked up at him. "Why would she think that?"

"You think I told her something?" His eyes widened, then he shook his head. "I didn't, Alana, I swear. That's just the way she is. She always thinks that someone is out to take something from her. You and I both know that it was just a ride home." He cleared his throat. "Not that I didn't want it to be more than that."

"What?" I stared at him.

"Look, I didn't make a move, did I?" He smiled. "That doesn't mean that I didn't want to. I've had enough of Sherry's jealousy, and I'll bet after tonight, you're over Mick. I know that now might not be the right time, but I'm just going to let you know that I'm interested." He locked his eyes to mine. "Anytime."

"Oh." I stared back at him, uncertain how to respond. Graham was interested in me?

"It's alright, you don't have to say anything right now." He shrugged. "Just think about it." He glanced at my notebook. "What are you working on here?"

"Nothing." I closed my notebook. "Graham, aren't you friends with Mick?"

"Sure I am. We're all friends on the team."

"Then you're friends with Ty too?" I met his eyes.

"Not exactly. He's kind of the new guy." He shrugged.

"I noticed that he never plays."

"Well, like I said, he's the new guy. Guys who have been on the team longer get first priority." He narrowed his eyes. "Is that what you really want to talk about? Football?"

"I guess I'm trying to figure out what is going on with Mick. I mean, is he usually so jealous?" I frowned. "I thought I knew him better than this."

I watched his reaction. Maybe something Graham said or did would reveal a little more truth about Mick's involvement with Coach Baker.

"He's been under a little pressure lately." He shrugged.

"What kind of pressure?" I searched his eyes.

"You know, just pressure." He turned in his chair so that his knees faced me, and lowered his voice. "He's always got something going on the side. Things with Coach Baker."

"I don't understand." My heart skipped a beat.

"I don't really either. Not all of it anyway. All I know is that the two of them are always alone together, always talking about something that Mick won't tell me anything about." He shook his head. "I've been trying to find out what, just to see if I can help Mick out. Something just doesn't feel right about it."

"What have you found out?" I held my breath. Was it possible that Graham knew about Coach Baker's activities?

"Nothing I can talk about here." He pursed his lips. "I mean, I just don't have enough information to prove anything at this point. I've been trying, but like I said, they're very secretive. I wouldn't want to say the wrong thing and have it get back to them." He glanced around the library. "Even quiet places like this have ears that are always listening."

"I'd like to hear more about this." I turned in my chair, so that my knees met his and held his gaze. "Anything you can tell me, I want to know."

"I thought you might." He scratched his cheek as he glanced at my notebook again. "That's what you're writing about, isn't it? Something about Coach Baker? That's what Sherry told me."

"How would Sherry know what I'm working on?" I narrowed my eyes.

"She said she had Hallie spy on you." He shrugged. "Anyway, you can trust me. I won't tell anyone about it. Really, we're pretty much on the same team with this." He rested one hand on one of my knees and continued to stare into my eyes. "The important question is, can I trust you, Alana?"

The heat of his touch on my knee mixed with the pounding of my heart to give me a generally sick feeling. I wanted to know everything that he did about Coach Baker, about Mick. I wanted one thing to turn out right that night, even if it meant that I had to ignore my own instincts.

"Yes, you can trust me. I'll do whatever it takes to get to the truth. Now tell me, what is Mick involved with in regards to Coach Baker?"

"I can't." He frowned, then glanced over his shoulder. "Not here. Can you meet me tomorrow afternoon? Outside of school grounds. It's the only way I can be sure that no one is listening in."

"Okay." I took a deep breath, then nodded. "Where?"

"At the little store down the street from here. You know it, don't you?" he whispered.

"I know it." I nodded.

"About four?" He met my eyes again.

"Yes, I'll be there." I watched as he pulled his hand away from my knee.

"Good." He smiled. "Don't worry, Alana, we're going to figure this out together. Like I said, we're on the same team."

"Right." I smiled in return, but as Graham left the library, I didn't feel as if I was on his team. In fact, I didn't feel as if I was on anyone's team. Hallie had been spying on me? Were my instincts so off that I didn't even know who was my friend and who wasn't? I had to face the fact that they might be. I'd managed to fall in love with Mick, after all, when he was involved in Coach Baker's unsavory activities. Maybe my judgment wasn't the best.

As I left the library, the weight of the day exhausted me. It was hard to believe that as the sun had risen that morning, I'd shared a kiss that I knew I would never forget with a person I thought was just right for me.

But now, I felt more alone than ever.

TWENTY-FOUR

After a restless night's sleep, I decided to get an early start to my day. I didn't want to lose any opportunity to find out the truth about Coach Baker. I hoped that by evening, I would know the facts.

As I made my way through the living room toward the door, a voice from the kitchen startled me.

"Alana." Cyndi frowned as I turned to face her.

"Sorry, Cyndi, I thought you would still be sleeping." I walked over to the kitchenette.

"Hey, are you okay?" Cyndi handed me a cup of coffee as she looked across the counter at me. "I feel like I've hardly seen you in so long and now you're trying to sneak out again."

"I'm not sneaking out." I took the cup of coffee. "Thanks for this. I'm just trying to get an early start."

"You know me, I don't pay much attention to rumors, but last night the dorm was buzzing with stuff about you and Graham." She shook her head. "That isn't true, is it?"

"No." I winced. "No, it's not true at all. Yesterday was rough. I don't even want to think about it." But that wasn't completely true. There was one thing that I couldn't stop thinking about. That kiss. Heat washed over me. I did my best to ignore it. "Cyndi, please don't worry about me. I'm fine."

"Okay." She sighed. "But if you ever want to talk about anything, you know I'm here."

"Thanks, Cyndi." I drank the coffee as fast as I could, then set the cup on the counter. "I've got this." I nodded to her, then hurried out the door.

I didn't have it. Not even close. But I wanted to pretend that I did.

When my phone rang, I saw that it was Mick and ignored it. I couldn't speak to him. At least, not until after I'd spoken to Graham.

Even the thought of Mick threatened to make me lose all of my resolve. Despite his jealous behavior the night before, my feelings for him hadn't faded. I knew if I heard his voice, my determination would crumble. I couldn't let that happen.

I walked in the direction of the library, ready to do some more research on Coach Baker. On my way, I noticed a familiar face. The moment I saw her, my muscles tensed. I could have just kept walking. I could have ignored her. But no matter how much I insisted, my feet would not continue to move.

"Hallie?" I watched as she smoothed down a flyer she'd just posted on the bulletin board in the courtyard.

"Alana." She smiled as she looked over at me. "How are you?"

"How am I?" I stared at her, unsure how to confront her.

"What's wrong?" She stepped closer. "You seem upset."

"I am upset." I crossed my arms as I studied her. "I thought we were friends."

"We are friends." She shook her head. "Is this about me getting kicked off the cheerleading squad? I told you, that wasn't your fault."

"I know it wasn't. Now I do." I frowned. "You don't have to

keep up the act. In fact, I'd rather you didn't." I lowered my voice as a few students walked past us. I didn't want to draw more attention than necessary.

"What act?" She crossed her arms as well. "What is this about? You're acting like you're angry with me."

"I am angry with you." I balled my hands into fists. I thought about all the times we'd talked and how she'd acted as if I was her friend. "I thought I could trust you."

"I don't understand." Her eyes widened. "Alana, you're going to have to be straight with me and tell me what's going on here."

"I just want to know—what did Sherry offer you to make you willing to spy on me?" I glared at her. "If you had told me, maybe I could have offered you something better."

"Spy on you?" She laughed. "You can't be serious."

"I am serious." My heart slammed against my chest. "It's nothing to laugh about. I thought you were my friend and the entire time you were reporting back to Sherry."

"That's not true!" She stared into my eyes. "Who told you that?"

"Why? So that you can tell Sherry that too?" I gritted my teeth. I wasn't going to have Graham in the crosshairs because he had told me the truth about Hallie. "It doesn't matter who told me, all that matters is that I know now. I'm not going to let you or anyone else get under my skin anymore. So you can report that back to Sherry!"

"Alana!" Hallie glared at me. "You've lost your mind. I would never spy for anyone and certainly not Sherry. She kicked me off the squad, remember? For being your friend!"

"At least that's the story that you told." My voice wavered. I had no idea if she was lying now or if she had been lying before. I thought I could tell when people were being dishonest, but now it was clear that I couldn't.

"It wasn't a story." Alana frowned. "I chose our friendship over the cheerleading squad and that was no easy task. But I just couldn't stand the thought of you being treated so unfairly. I thought if you couldn't be a real part of the squad, then it didn't matter if I couldn't be either." She squeezed her eyes shut tight and took a sharp breath. "But I guess that was just me being stupid. Because it seems to me that you don't care at all about what I did for you."

"Hallie." My heart softened as I heard the shiver in her voice. When she opened her eyes again, I detected the gleam of tears. "I'm sorry. Someone told me that you were spying for Sherry."

"And you believed that person?" She sniffed, then wiped at her eyes. "I guess whoever it was must be far more trustworthy than me."

I thought about Graham and the things he'd confided in me. Was he trustworthy? I never would have considered him to be trustworthy before. But now, I had no idea who to trust.

"Hallie, I really am sorry." I reached for her hand. "Things have been so crazy, but I never should have doubted you."

"You're right, you shouldn't have." She pursed her lips and took a step back. "But I guess now I know where I stand with you."

"Hallie, please. I'm just trying to figure everything out at this point."

"I think you've got it figured out just fine." She sighed then turned and walked away from me, calling over her shoulder as she left. "It's important to know who your friends are, Alana. If you don't know that I'm one of them, then maybe we weren't ever friends to begin with."

I opened my mouth to call out to her but closed it instead. What could I say? An apology wouldn't be enough if she really hadn't been spying for Sherry. If she had been, then this might just be another con.

My stomach flipped as tears filled my eyes. Not knowing whom I could trust left me spinning from one thought to another. Maybe Graham was lying. But why would he? Maybe Sherry had lied to him, but why would she? Somehow, I'd gotten myself caught up in something that left me no solid ground to stand on.

My cell phone rang again. I saw Mick's name and hit ignore. Another person whom I had no idea if I could trust.

Seconds later, Maby's name flickered across the screen. I ignored her call as well.

I needed to clear my head. The only way to get out of this tailspin of confusion and suspicion was to get to the truth, and if that meant losing friendships along the way, then that was what I had to do.

I continued on to the library and spent the hour before classes started researching Coach Baker. I found that he had been transferred between a few different schools before he'd ended up at Oak Brook Academy. Why? Had he had trouble at those other schools? I decided I would try to find out more at lunch.

As I walked to class, I wondered if Mick might hunt me down. A big part of me wanted him to. I wanted to look into those warm eyes and feel his strong arms around me. I wanted to rest my head against his chest and breathe in the scent of his cologne. I wanted that to be the only thing on my mind.

But instead, as I stepped into my first class of the day, what preoccupied me the most was whom I could trust.

TWENTY-FIVE

It was impossible for me to concentrate in any of my classes. As the day marched by, I found myself stuck in the first moments of it. I'd woken up to thoughts about Mick, to the memory of his lips on mine, and that was the memory that lingered in my mind throughout the morning.

I wished that I'd never figured out anything about Coach Baker. I wished that Mick and I could just be two people at a school, two people that were free to enjoy one another's company. Instead, I was someone who knew too much and he was someone who was far too involved in things he shouldn't have been. I winced at the thought and tried to focus on the easel in front of me.

Art class was one of my least favorite subjects. I just didn't have that kind of creativity. I noticed Apple's painting as she was seated only a few easels away from me. I'd never really paid attention to anyone else's artwork, but now that I had seen her masterpiece on the ceiling of the hideout, I was curious to see what else she could create. There was no question in my mind that she was talented.

The landscape that she created on the blank space of the

canvas reminded me of every beautiful place I'd ever been and perhaps some that I had yet to see. I didn't know much about art, but I knew that I liked her painting.

"Stop," she whispered without turning her head toward me.

"Me?" I whispered back.

The two students between us had headphones on. The art teacher encouraged students to listen to music of their choice while they painted.

"Yes, you." She still refused to look at me.

"Stop what?"

"Stop staring. It's very distracting."

"How can you tell?"

She sighed, then finally looked at me. "I just can. Okay?"

"Okay, I'm sorry." I frowned as I looked back at my barely touched canvas.

"You should try painting." She stood up and walked over to me. "It can be a really good emotional release."

"Thanks, but it just doesn't work that way for me."

"Have you tried?" She pointed to my paintbrush. "It doesn't have to be anything, you know. It doesn't have to have shape or any specific color, it can just be movement."

"Movement?" That idea drew my interest. All my life I'd found comfort in movement, in the sensation of weightlessness that came from flipping through the air. I'd never thought about trying to paint that feeling.

"Just remember, the only rule in art is that you have to be part of it." She smiled as she met my eyes. "If you can't open your heart, then nothing will spill out. Opening your heart can feel dangerous at first, but once you do it, you'll wonder how you ever survived with it closed so tight."

"My heart isn't closed tight." I pursed my lips.

"Just offering some advice." She gave me a small smile, then returned to her canvas. "Just please stop staring."

I sighed and looked back at the canvas in front of me. I'd been so fixated on Mick, on Coach Baker, and even on Graham, that I hadn't even though about moving lately. I couldn't exactly cartwheel through the classroom, but maybe I could try to take Apple's advice.

I picked up a paintbrush and began to swipe it across the canvas. Instead of going in any certain direction or drawing any particular shape, I flicked it in the way that my body snapped into action. Then I swept it back with the smooth rush of a backflip.

As I continued to spread the paint and visualize the movements that always gave me comfort and a sense of freedom, I finally began to relax. My muscles ached as the tension began to leave them. I'd been so wound up that I hadn't even noticed how tight everything in my body had been.

I recalled Mick's massage—the way his fingertips dug down and spread warmth that eased the pain. The memory made me dizzy and I included that swirl and spike in the painting as well.

By the time the class came to an end, my canvas was covered in swipes of paint in all different colors in all different directions. And right in the middle was a swirl and a spike.

"Impressive." Apple peered over my shoulder. "See? Beautiful things happen when you open your heart."

"Thanks, Apple." I smiled at her, then tilted my head to the side. I wasn't sure that I could call my painting beautiful, but it was certainly something to look at.

When the bell rang for lunch, I rushed out of the classroom. It wasn't until I was almost to the cafeteria that I realized I'd left my backpack behind, along with my notebook full of evidence.

Annoyed, I ran back. When I stepped inside what I expected to be an empty classroom, I spotted Mick right away. It was impossible not to, with his broad shoulders and towering height. He stood in front of my painting, nearly blocking it from view.

My heart skipped a beat as I realized that the only way to get to my backpack was to face him. I didn't have time to think about how to avoid it, as an instant later he turned around to face me.

"Lala, I was hoping I would catch you. But you'd already left." He glanced back at the painting. "Did you do this?"

"Yes." I took a hesitant step into the classroom.

Did I want to be alone with him? Every nerve in my body indicated that I did, but my brain warned me that it was a dangerous idea. Dangerous because I couldn't be trusted not to grab him and kiss him.

"It's mesmerizing." He shook his head. "I didn't know you were an artist." He turned back toward me and met my eyes. "I guess there's a lot I don't know about you."

"We haven't had much time to get to know one another." I took another step further into the room. Now there was only one easel between us.

He shortened that distance when he took a step closer to me.

"There are things I want to know." He continued to hold my gaze. "Like why you won't answer my calls. Why you insist on keeping secrets from me."

"Me?" I couldn't hold back a laugh. "You think I'm the one keeping secrets?"

"I don't know what you mean." He took that last step between us.

"Mick." My breath caught in my throat the moment I detected the scent of his cologne.

"I'm not the one taking secret rides with Graham." He caught one of my hands with his and stared hard into my eyes.

"That didn't have to be a secret, unless there was a reason for it to be."

"It wasn't a secret." I glared at him. "Because it didn't need to be. Because I don't need to report to you who I do or don't take rides with. Because you should know that if I'm with you, then there is no reason to wonder what might have happened between me and Graham."

"Are you?" He caught my other hand and the small amount of distance between us was smothered as he shifted closer, so close that I could just tip my head and taste those lips I'd been yearning for. "With me?" He lowered his voice to a whisper, his breath tickling along my cheek.

"Mick." My heart pounded as I did my best to resist caressing his lips with my own. I wanted nothing more than to wrap my arms around him and sweep away the pain that I saw in those beautiful eyes. But what if it was all lies? "Like you said, we don't know each other very well."

"I know enough to know that I want to be with you. If you don't know that much, then maybe that's my answer." He released my hands then stepped back away from me. "I want to be with you, Alana, I've made that clear from the very start. I can't make it any more clear. Yeah, I got jealous. Because Graham and I have issues to begin with. I wouldn't put it past him to try something with you just to get to me. You don't know him like I do. You can't trust him."

"Nothing happened." I bit into my bottom lip as he took another step away from me. How I wanted to reach out and pull him back. I wanted to grab hold of him before he could disappear forever.

"I know you're hiding something. I don't know what it is." He clenched his jaw, then shook his head. "But whatever it is, it's obviously more important than what's between us. Just do me a favor, don't trust Graham. Okay?" He searched my eyes.

"He's not a good person to be around. Just trust me enough to believe that."

"Mick, please." I reached for his hand, but he turned away before I could grasp it.

"I'm here, when you want me, Lala." He glanced back at me. "When you trust me."

TWENTY-SIX

It took all my strength to resist the urge to chase after Mick, to insist that I was ready right then and would believe anything he said.

I couldn't. Not yet. Not until I spoke to Graham and found out what he had to say.

I decided to avoid the cafeteria and grabbed something from the vending machine instead. I couldn't face Maby after I'd avoided her calls and texts. I couldn't risk running into Mick again.

Instead, I sat on one of the benches in the courtyard and read through the notes I'd made in my notebook. I was so close I could taste it. Mick had warned me not to trust Graham and I'd heard the desperation in his voice, but that wasn't enough to keep me away from him.

Wasn't it possible that Mick only wanted me to back off because he thought I was getting too close to finding out the truth? If that was the case, then it was all the more reason for me to go through with the meeting with Graham. I had to at least hear him out.

As I flipped to the next page in my notebook, I heard the

grinding of wheels against the cobblestone courtyard. I glanced up in time to see Ty whiz past me.

"Ty!" I waved to him.

He skidded to a stop and turned back to face me. "Yeah?"

"What are you doing?"

He looked at me, then looked at his skateboard, then looked back at me. "Riding?"

"Yes, I can see that, but why aren't you at lunch?" I stood up from the bench.

"Eh, I look to blow off some steam in the middle of the day. Sometimes this place can be a little too much for me." He pushed his hair away from his eyes. "Everyone's so..." He paused, then shrugged. "Perfect."

"Trust me, it's far from perfect around here." I glanced toward the school as I heard the bell for the end of lunch. "Could we meet up later? Before dinner? I have some more questions I want to ask you."

"I don't know." He picked up his skateboard. "Homework, practice, you know."

"Right. But I only need a few minutes. I promise." I smiled.

"Okay." He nodded. "Just for a few minutes."

"Thanks, Ty."

He walked off before I could say another word. I noticed the way he avoided interacting with the other students he passed. Ty was more isolated from the rest of the kids at school than I realized.

As the end of the school day approached, my nerves were on edge. What if Graham didn't show up for our meeting? What if he did? What if he told me things about Mick that I couldn't ignore?

My stomach twisted with a mixture of fear and anticipation. Would I stay true to my story and the desire to expose the truth or would I do what I could to protect someone that I cared for more deeply than I thought was possible?

The final bell rang and I bolted out of my seat. I didn't want to waste any time getting to the meet-up spot. Even though it was a little early, I preferred to be there first—to see Graham coming.

As I left the school grounds, I heard the laughter and conversations behind me.

Most of the students at Oak Brook Academy didn't have much to be worried about. They enjoyed their excellent education, the opportunity to create lasting friendships, and the unrivaled arts and science programs that the school offered.

Most, but not me.

I walked down the sidewalk with the weight of the world on my shoulders. Maybe in the future I would get paid for these moments of stress and uncertainty. Maybe I would get my name in a newspaper or a magazine. Maybe I would even win an award. But right then, the only thing I wanted to win was the truth. As much as I wanted to be with Mick, he was right. I could never truly be with him if he didn't trust me.

As I approached the shop, I heard footsteps behind me. When I glanced over my shoulder, I didn't see anyone.

Had I imagined it?

I began to walk again. This time I was sure that I heard someone behind me. I turned quickly to face whoever it was, but again there was no one there.

"You're losing it, Alana." I rolled my eyes and stepped into the shop.

Maybe this would be it. Maybe Graham would clear Mick's name, maybe I would be able to open my heart as Apple had suggested and embrace Mick and the undeniable connection between us. I hoped that would be the case.

While I waited for Graham to show up, I browsed through

the magazine and newspaper section. I thought about my future, and for the first time, I didn't just think about working as a reporter.

I thought about Mick's being by my side. I thought about marrying him and starting a family with him. My mind spun as I realized that was exactly what I wanted. Yes, it was a little unrealistic to think it would happen when we were so young and had barely gotten to know one another, but that didn't change the fact that I wanted it. The fantasy filled me with a sense of excitement that I'd never experienced before.

What if that was the life that I wanted, and my choice not to trust Mick had taken that life from me before I even had the chance to dream about it?

The door to the shop swung open. I turned toward it and saw Graham step inside. He met my eyes, then gestured for me to follow him as he walked through the store.

I felt a little uneasy as I recalled Mick's warnings. Still, I needed to know what Graham had to say. As I followed him, he pushed his way through a rear door and out into an alley behind the shop.

Again, I hesitated. I had thought meeting at the store was a fairly safe place, but now we were alone.

"Are you coming or not?" He flashed a grin at me as I stood in the doorway.

"Why here?" I remained half-inside and half-outside of the shop.

"What I have to tell you isn't something that can be over-heard by anyone. I think we're safe here, but I can't be too careful." He looked into my eyes. "Do you want to risk expulsion?"

"No, definitely not." I stepped the rest of the way out into the alley. "What do you have to tell me?"

"I think it's time you knew the truth, Alana. Even if that means putting myself at risk." He frowned. "But before I can do that. I have to know that I can trust you. You have to tell me what you've found out so far about Coach Baker."

I stared back into his eyes. I could understand his desire to be able to trust me. But I wasn't sure whether it was wise to tell him the truth.

"You first." I crossed my arms.

"That's not how this works." He glared at me.

"Start with Mick." I forced the name from between my lips. My chest filled with dread as I wondered what he might say. "How is he involved in all this?"

"You know already, don't you?" He offered a faint smirk. "You know more than I thought."

"Just tell me the truth, Graham. I need to know." I walked up to him, determined not to let him avoid my questions. "I'll tell you everything, but first you have to tell me that."

"Yeah, Mick's involved." He narrowed his eyes. "He's definitely involved. He's the mastermind of it all."

"Of what exactly?" I tried to take a breath, though it seemed impossible.

"Now it's your turn." His face neared mine. "Now you need to tell me everything that you know."

"What are they doing exactly?" I frowned.

"Enough!"

I jumped at the sound of his shout. His expression had shifted from determined to frustrated. "Graham?"

"I'm not waiting anymore." He glared into my eyes. "You'd better start talking, right now."

TWENTY-SEVEN

"I'm done with this." I stepped back and turned toward the door of the shop. As my heart raced, I realized that I was in danger. Graham wasn't there to tell me the truth, he was there to find out what I knew.

Before I could reach the door, he grabbed me by the arm.

"Not so fast." He tugged me back toward him. "Listen, you need to consider this your warning. You need to back off!"

"Back off?" I turned around to face him as fear sent a shiver up my spine. "You were involved in this the whole time? How could I not see it?"

"It doesn't surprise me." He smirked. "You think you're so smart, don't you, Alana? You've been picking away at Coach Baker all year. Why do you think Mick showed any interest in you?" He searched my eyes as his smirk spread into a smile. "Why do you think he wanted anything to do with you?"

"Are you saying that Mick was in on this the whole time?" My stomach twisted at the thought.

"I'm saying that he was told to find out whatever he could from you, no matter what it took." He raised an eyebrow as he studied me. "You didn't really think he liked you, did you?" He chuckled.

"I don't believe you." I spat the words out, but the truth was, I was already crumbling inside. I did believe him. It explained why Mick had been involved in my life at all. It explained why he had been so relentless about getting close to me. It wasn't because he was interested in me, it was because I was getting too close to the truth.

"Fine, don't." He shrugged. "Maybe you're right. Maybe he does have a thing for you. It doesn't really matter now, because if you come out with anything that you've discovered, Mick is going to be one of the first people that goes down." He stared straight into my eyes. "If you keep looking into this—if you write any articles about it—your days at Oak Brook Academy will be numbered."

"You can't threaten me." I glared at him. "I haven't done anything wrong. I won't be kicked out of school."

"There are other ways to make someone leave." He grabbed my arm again.

This time his grip was so tight that I cried out in pain.

"Get your hands off of her!" Mick jumped out from the shadows of the alley and slammed into Graham. The pair wrestled down to the ground.

I jumped back and watched as they rolled around, each trying to throw a punch at the other.

"Stop!" I gasped and tried to grab onto Graham. He threw me back easily and aimed a punch for Mick's face.

"Enough!" The door of the shop slammed shut. The owner glared at the three of us and shouted again. "If you don't get out of here right now, I'm calling the cops!"

Graham broke free of Mick's grasp and bolted down the alley.

I held out my hand to Mick to help him up. He grabbed it and stood up.

"I'm sorry." He glanced at the store owner.

"Just get out of here!" He pointed down the alley.

"We're going, we're going." Mick wrapped his arm around my shoulder.

Confusion flooded through me as he guided me down the alley. Had he intervened to protect me or had he intervened to protect himself? Was Graham telling the truth about the reason he'd been interested in me?

As soon as we reached the end of the alley, I pulled away from his arm.

"Are you okay?" He caught my wrist. "Did he hurt you?" He ran his fingertips along the length of my forearm.

"I'm fine. He didn't hurt me." I pulled my arm away from him. "Were you following me?"

"I was." His cheeks flushed. "I was worried about you. And it turns out I had good reason to be. Didn't I tell you not to go near Graham?"

"Mick, you've told me a lot of things." I crossed my arms as I studied him. "I just have no idea what's been true and what's been a lie."

"You can't tell me that you believed him?" Mick's eyes widened. "Do you really think I would do something like that to you?"

"I don't know what to think. I don't know what to believe." I backed away as tears flooded my eyes. "All I know is that you're caught up in something that you shouldn't be."

"I can explain that." He crossed the distance between us and reached for my hand.

"No." I stepped out of his reach. "Don't. Please. I don't want to hear any more lies."

"So that's it then?" He balled his hands into fists. "After all this, you're just going to believe Graham over me?"

"What am I supposed to believe?" My voice rose and trembled as I tried to speak through raging emotions. "Graham said you were told to get close to me. Is that true?"

"It's not!" He stepped closer to me.

I stepped back and found a wall behind me. "Mick." My heart skipped a beat as he stepped even closer. "I saw you. I saw you give Coach Baker an envelope full of money." I looked at him intently, hoping that he'd have some kind of explanation.

"So, you were following me?" He took a slow breath and shook his head. "You're standing here accusing me of conning you this whole time, but it was you, wasn't it?" His eyes widened as he stared at me. "You weren't ever really interested in me. I was just part of your investigation!"

"Mick, it's not like that." I stumbled over my words, startled by his discovery.

"Yes, it is." He walked backwards as he continued to stare at me. "It's exactly like that. How could I be so stupid? That's what you've been hiding this whole time. I thought you actually liked me."

"Mick, please." I tried to wrap my arm around his waist, but he jerked out of my grasp.

"No, don't even try it. I can't believe I was this stupid!" He shook his head. "It's all just been a job to you."

"It hasn't been." I drew a sharp breath. "If you will just listen to me for a second!"

"Why? So you can lie to me some more?" He glared at me. "So you can make me look even more ridiculous?"

"As if you weren't lying to me?" I glared back at him. "Graham told me that you were involved. He told me that you're the mastermind behind all this. And you're going to act like I did something wrong here?"

"Graham, Graham, Graham. If he tells you something, then it must be true? Oh, I forgot, you trust him more than you trust me. You go for rides in cars with him. You have secret meetings with him. He must be telling you the truth." He waved his hand through the air. "Don't try to get out of this. You know what you did." His jaw clenched as he took another slow breath. "You used me. That's all." He turned and strode away.

Panic washed over me and demanded that I chase after him. But I didn't. I wouldn't.

Maybe he was right. Maybe I had used him. But he also hadn't denied being involved with Coach Baker. He hadn't said he was innocent.

With Graham's warning still hanging in my mind, I wondered if it would be safe to go through with publishing the article. At this point, I doubted that Mick would ever be interested in me again. I didn't even know if he ever really was in the first place. But Graham knew I knew too much now.

The only way to keep myself safe was to get to the truth and make it known.

TWENTY-EIGHT

I walked slowly back toward Oak Brook Academy. Several things had changed in the span of less than an hour. Coach Baker now likely knew that I was investigating him. Graham had proven to be quite a threat. Mick.

"Oh, Mick." I sighed as I reached the gates of the school. I didn't want things to be over between us, but I didn't have much choice. He wasn't wrong about my betrayal. I wasn't wrong about his. I still didn't know everything there was to know about his involvement with Coach Baker and he hadn't exactly volunteered to tell me.

Still in a daze, I almost forgot about my meeting with Ty until my phone buzzed with a reminder. I headed for the courtyard, where I knew that he liked to spend time on his skateboard.

The more I thought about it, the more I realized how little I actually knew about Ty. He wasn't exactly shy, he was just quiet. He didn't offer up a lot about himself. What I did know about him, I'd learned from Mick.

I winced at the memory of our last moments together. Maybe I shouldn't have been upset, maybe I should have just asked for his forgiveness. But what good would that do? It was clear now that he was involved with Coach Baker. Could I ever forgive him for that?

"Hey." Ty walked up to me with his skateboard tucked under his arm. "I thought maybe you weren't coming."

"Sorry, I got caught up in something." I frowned as I met his eyes. "Actually, I got caught between Graham and Mick."

"Huh." He glanced around at the empty courtyard then looked back at me. "What? Were they fighting over you?" He grinned.

"Not exactly." I cleared my throat. "Ty, I need you to tell me the truth about some things."

"Alright." He shrugged. "I like to be straight with people."

"Good." I took a deep breath. "I know that Mick is involved in something with Coach Baker and Graham. You two seem close. Can you tell me anything about it?"

"Ah, I don't know if I should." He rubbed the back of his neck. "Mick's been good to me, you know."

"If there is any way that I can help Mick, I'm going to find it." I lowered my voice. "But the truth is going to come out one way or another. I'd rather hear from someone who really knows Mick than someone who is out to hurt him."

"I'm out of my element here." He ruffled his fingers through his hair. "It's pretty clear I don't belong. I'm not sure that me rocking the boat is the wisest idea."

"Ty. I need you to be bold." I put my hands on his shoulders and looked into his eyes. "The only way I can help Mick is if I find out what is really going on with him. I can't promise you that there's no risk, but I can promise you that we can work together to help Mick—if that's what you want."

"Okay then." He stepped back so that my hands dropped away from his shoulders. "It's not that I don't want to help, it's just that I don't know if that's what you're going to do. How do I know I can trust you?"

"You don't."

"That's reassuring." He frowned.

"No one else is here offering to help Mick, right?" I shook my head. "Without your help, he's just going to be left dangling. Do you think Graham or Coach Baker are going to do anything to help him?"

"No." He narrowed his eyes. "Not a chance."

"So tell me." I gazed at him. "Please, Ty."

"I don't know everything. I just know what Mick told me." He glanced around the courtyard again, then spoke in a quieter voice. "After a couple weeks of the coach not letting me play, Mick told me that the only people that play are the people that pay."

"What does that mean?" I searched his expression for any hints.

"It means that if you want to be on the field, you or your parents have to pay quite a bit of money to Coach Baker. Obviously, I can't pay a dime." He shrugged. "Mick told me because he wanted me to know it wasn't about my skill. It was about money. Like everything."

"I'm sorry about that. It's not right." I crossed my arms. "It's not how this school is usually run. It sounds to me like Coach Baker is running his own side business to line his pockets. Did Mick say that he was involved?"

"No, he didn't say."

"Did you think about going to the principal?" I shook my head. "Maybe we could put an end to all of this."

"No." His tone grew sharper. "Mick warned me not to cross Coach Baker. He said that he knew it was unfair, but that I was better off just dealing with it. He was just trying to help me out."

"I'll bet." I frowned. Was he? Or was he trying to protect himself? "Ty, do you have any proof of this? Anything that might help me to catch Coach Baker?"

"No. Nothing." He glanced around again. "Maybe you should just leave this alone, Alana. I know that might be hard for you, but it sounds like whatever Mick is into is something you don't want to be involved in."

"Maybe." I sighed. "Thanks for your time, Ty. I appreciate it."

"Good, you can thank me by keeping my name out of all this. Got it?" He locked his eyes to mine.

"Got it." I nodded.

He dropped his skateboard on the ground, then took off on it.

I walked back toward the dormitory and tried to straighten a few things out in my mind. Now I knew what that list of names and dollar amounts referred to. That was what Coach Baker charged his players to have game time. I couldn't let him get away with it.

Graham had warned me to stay out of it, Mick had too and now Ty. But that wasn't even an option. I couldn't let something so unfair continue to happen right under my nose in a school that I loved. But before I could do anything, I had to make sure that I had all the evidence that I needed. I couldn't risk Coach Baker's finding a way to talk himself out of it. I needed my evidence to be solid.

As I stepped into my dorm room, I was relieved to see that Cyndi wasn't there. She had her own life, with her own activities. In the quiet, I could really dig into the article I wanted to finish and publish as soon as possible.

I sat down at my desk and flipped open my notebook. As I began to read through it, I shuddered at what the consequences of publishing this article might be. I didn't have permission from

Mr. Raynaud and I could only imagine how the school administration would react. But this was why being a journalist was so important to me.

When my phone buzzed, I ignored it at first. Then I heard it buzz again. I glanced at the screen and saw Maby's name bounce across it.

I closed my eyes, then sent the call to voicemail. Wasn't she the one that had assured me that Mick was such a good guy? How could I even trust her after everything that had happened?

My phone buzzed again. This time I saw Mick's name.

"Not a chance." I glared at the phone.

Maybe Mick had a right to be angry at me, but I had a right to be angry too. Even though I didn't think I could trust him, I still didn't want to be the reason that he was kicked out of school.

Was my loyalty to him misplaced? Was I still falling for his con? I had no idea whom to trust.

Maby might have known about it all along. She seemed to know everything about everyone. Hallie might have been spying on me from the start. Maybe even Cyndi was part of it all. I shivered at the thought.

If Mick had been lying to me the whole time, would that kiss have felt so amazing? Would the thought of his arms around me still leave me so dizzy with desire?

Maybe I couldn't even trust myself.

TWENTY-NINE

An hour later, my neck was sore and I had run out of ways to try to keep Mick out of the article.

Although I had the pictures of the names of the players and the dollar amounts, that didn't mean anything without something to prove the purpose of the list. My having witnessed Mick handing Coach Baker that money was the only evidence that linked the activities together. If I didn't include that, then there was no chance that the article would have the impact I was hoping for.

I started to type out a few paragraphs about what I'd seen, but every time my finger moved toward the "m" key, I pulled it back. Could I really just hang him out to dry? Could I risk his entire future?

Not without talking to him first. I picked up my phone and looked over the last call I'd received from him. He hadn't tried to call again. Would he even agree to meet with me? Could I trust myself alone with him?

Just the thought of seeing him again sent my heart racing.

"Stop, Alana, just stop." I winced. "You need to focus on the article, not on your crush."

I bit into my bottom lip as I began to type out a text to him. If he agreed to meet me, then we could discuss what his role in all this was. If not, then I would feel that I had a final answer from him.

MEET ME AT THE HIDEOUT? Fifteen minutes?

I THOUGHT the hideout would be the safest place for us to talk. I didn't doubt what Graham said about there being ears all around the school. But there, it could just be us. At least, I thought it could. Would he be willing?

I closed my computer and sat back in my chair.

I wanted the article out by the morning. I didn't want to have too much time to talk myself out of it. I didn't want to give Graham and Coach Baker too much opportunity to threaten me again. I had to get this settled, no matter what it took.

As minutes crept by, I began to convince myself that Mick was not going to text me back. He had made his decision and he didn't want anything to do with me. I couldn't really blame him. The truth was, I shouldn't be interested in him either, not after what he'd done. He'd obviously helped line Coach Baker's pockets and hadn't turned to the principal or anyone else for help.

Just as I was about to give up completely, my phone buzzed. I glanced at the screen, bracing myself for his rejection. Instead, the text that he sent agreed to the meeting.

My heart pounded. That meant I had to leave right then to meet him. It meant that I didn't have time to prepare for what it would be like to see him again, knowing everything that I did now. I barely had time to pull my hair back in a ponytail and toss my phone into my pocket.

As nervous as I was to see him again, I was also excited. He'd agreed to meet me. That had to mean something, didn't it? It had to mean that he wasn't ready to walk away.

Unless he had another reason for meeting me. Unless he intended to threaten me, just as Graham had.

I pushed the thought away. Mick would never hurt me.

As I walked across the school grounds in the direction of the hideout, I rehearsed what I would say.

"Mick, I understand that you're upset, but that's not what we need to talk about right now. Right now, we need to figure out this situation with Coach Baker."

Yes, I sounded professional and calm. He would respond well to that. He would want to discuss things with me, help me to clear his name. At least, I hoped that he would.

But what if things turned out to be different? What if there was no way to clear his name? Would that stop me from publishing the article?

I rehearsed the words again as I rounded a corner and approached the buildings at the edge of the property. Only then did I consider whether someone might be following me.

I glanced over my shoulder. No sign of anyone. No footsteps. I held my breath and listened even closer. Still nothing.

I continued on to the building. As I reached the door, I wondered if he would be inside. Maybe he had agreed to meet me with no intention of actually showing up.

The door swung open, a hand shot out and pulled me inside in the same moment that the door slammed shut.

"Shh!" Mick put his finger to his lips as he stared into my eyes. "Did anyone see you come in here?"

"No, I don't think so." I pulled out of his grasp as my heart raced.

"I'm sorry, but we have to be careful." He peeked through one of the windows. "Are you sure no one saw you?"

"I checked to see if someone was following me. I'm getting used to that." I placed my hands on my hips as I looked at him. "We're alone, Mick. Just you and me."

"I know." He looked back at me and his eyes collided with mine. "You asked me to come, I came."

"I needed to talk to you." I studied his every movement, looking for a sign of the deceitful person that Graham claimed he was. "I want to hear the truth—from you."

"That's a strange request, coming from you." He crossed his arms as he stared back at me. "Here I thought you wanted to meet so that you could apologize to me."

"Why should I apologize when you're the criminal?"

"Criminal?" He glared at me. "I wouldn't go that far."

"What do you call helping a coach sell positions on the football team?" I crossed my arms as well.

"Who told you that?" His eyes widened. "Was it Ty?"

"I figured it out. Now, do you want to tell me why you did it? I mean, I did think that I'd gotten to know you pretty well and this is the last thing I expected from you." I held my breath and hoped he would tell me that none of it was true.

"I didn't have a choice, alright?" He sighed as he ran his hands back through his hair. "My stepdad lost his business. He lost everything on a bad investment. All the money we had was gone. I was going to have to leave school and lose any chance at getting into a good college." He closed his eyes and frowned. "I know it's not much of an excuse. I just wanted to quit. I wanted to walk away from everything. But I didn't have that option either. My mother and stepdad insisted that I stay. Coach Baker told them that because of my talent, he would keep me on as a scholarship student. That's what he told them." He opened his eyes and looked at me. "But that's not what he told me. He said that in order for me to stay I would have to help him with some things. I thought he meant cleaning the locker rooms or packing up equipment. I was fine with that. But that's not what he meant."

"He wanted your help collecting money from the other players?" I watched as he began to pace.

"Yes. I told him no. I told him that I would never do something like that. He said he would have me expelled then and that would eliminate any chance of my getting into a good school. Not only that, he would make sure that my stepdad could never open his business again." He turned to face me. "I don't expect you to understand, Alana. I started out with nothing. My mother has worked so hard and she's had to go back to working a couple of jobs just to make ends meet. I thought staying in this school, getting into a good college—it was the only thing I could offer either of them to help them. My stepdad came into my life and made it so much better. I just didn't want to let them down."

"Mick." I sighed.

"I know. It's wrong." He clenched his hands at his sides. "I know there's no excuse."

"I can see how you got caught up in all of it, Mick. He didn't really give you a choice." I bit into my bottom lip. "You couldn't find a way out."

THIRTY

"That's why I started reading your articles. I could tell that you were onto something. That got my attention. I was curious about you." He stared into my eyes. "I don't know if you'll ever believe me, but none of it was a con. None of it. I thought maybe you could help at first, but I couldn't risk telling you the truth. I didn't want you to get trapped under Coach Baker's thumb like I was. That's why I hid it from you."

"I'm not afraid of him." I narrowed my eyes.

"You should be." He shook his head. "He has ways of making you do whatever he wants."

"Maybe some people. But not me. He doesn't have anything on me and I'll make sure that he gets exactly what he deserves." I frowned as I studied him. "I just didn't want you to get caught in the middle of it all, Mick. I knew that you were a good guy."

"You believe me?" He met my eyes.

"I think I do, yes. But that's not what matters right now. What matters right now is getting the truth out there."

"No, you can't." He grasped my shoulders as he looked at me. "It's too dangerous. You can't expose him."

"I have no choice." I slipped my arms around his waist and held him close to me for the split-second that he allowed it.

"Of course you have a choice! Just like you had a choice when you decided that I should be part of your investigation." He shoved his hands into his pockets.

"You're right." I tried to meet his eyes, but he looked sharply away. "I did want to get information from you. I did see you and Coach Baker exchange that envelope. I also heard the way he spoke to you. I know that he has control over you. I know that none of this was your fault."

"Do you?" He glanced at me.

"I do. That's why I don't want you to be hurt in all this. But in order to prevent that, I need something—some kind of proof—to show what Coach Baker has really been up to."

"And that's still all this is about for you, isn't it?" He licked his lips as he shook his head. "Just the story."

"No, Mick. That's not all it's about." I wrapped my hand around his wrist and held on tight. "Mick, I care about you. I didn't expect that to happen. I'm sorry that I haven't been completely honest with you—"

"No." He stepped back and brushed my hand away. "You haven't been honest with me at all. I'll get you your proof. But know this." He met my eyes. "All I wanted to do was to protect you this entire time. All I ever wanted to do was keep you safe."

As he brushed past me and out the door, the skin of his arm briefly grazed mine. Desire rippled through me, followed by dread. The way he walked away, with sharp and determined strides, without even a quick glance back over his shoulder, made it clear that he wanted nothing to do with me.

I couldn't brave stepping outside. Not yet. Not when my heart ached the way it did. I had been so angry at him, so certain that he had been the one doing something wrong, when the truth was, I had betrayed him more than he ever could have betrayed me.

I flopped back on the cushions that lined the floor and looked up at the ceiling. For a few minutes I lost myself in Apple's painting. She found beauty wherever she was. She even taught me how to find it by opening my heart. But I thought that was what I had tried to do.

Instead of finding beauty, I'd found only heartbreak. I didn't want to feel this kind of pain. I curled up and closed my eyes as tears slipped down my cheeks. I thought of that fantasy life I had briefly let myself imagine. I didn't want it to be over before it even had the chance to get started.

I looked back up at the ceiling and recalled the kiss that Mick and I had shared on the roof. It was more than I ever imagined it could be. It was so powerful that I could still feel his warmth on my lips and the tingle that it left under my skin. I wanted to experience it again, not just once, but hundreds of times.

How had I let things get so out of control?

When I heard an engine nearby, I forced myself out of my daze. I had to get out of the building before anyone found me there. I watched as the security guard drove past, then I stepped out through the door. I wouldn't have this place anymore either. This place belonged to Mick. It was a gift that he'd given me that I would have to give back.

As I walked back toward the dormitories, I tried to think of ways to get him to forgive me. What if I proved to him that I really did care about him? But how? Anything I said or did—I knew he wouldn't trust. He'd always wonder if I really meant it.

I pushed open the door to my dorm room and found Cyndi sitting cross-legged on the sofa.

"Hey, Alana." She smiled at me. "Mick just dropped you off

a present." She waved a large yellow envelope in the air and grinned. "It looks like things are going pretty well."

"Thanks." I couldn't even muster a smile as I took the envelope. I didn't have the energy to explain to her everything that had happened. All I wanted to do was curl up in bed and forget that I even existed.

When my phone rang, with Maby's name on the ID, I turned it off. I didn't want to hear it anymore.

It would never be Mick calling, and that was all that mattered at the moment.

THIRTY-ONE

Instead of surrendering to my desire to curl up in bed, I sat down on the edge of it and opened the envelope. As I poured the papers out onto the bed, I noticed that some were hand-written documents, while others were photographs.

As I read over the notes, I began to see a pattern. Mick had kept track of everything that Coach Baker had asked him to do. He hadn't been lying to me when he said that he didn't want to be involved in this. He'd been keeping a paper trail in an attempt to prove what Coach Baker was up to. It was more than enough to publish my article.

The photographs showed Coach Baker with envelopes of cash, with individual players, and even with some parents. I knew that I could make a good enough case to force the school to look into it.

As I began to scan in the documents and photographs, I thought about how brave it was of Mick to document things this way. Even though he knew he could lose so much, he'd still tried to do the right thing. That was a quality that made him even more attractive to me. But he would never feel the same way about me.

I had deceived him. I couldn't deny that.

But our entire relationship had been influenced by people around us. By Sherry lying to him about pushing me into the pool. By Graham pretending to be my friend to find out what I was investigating. It had been tested from the very beginning by lies and maybe that meant it never really had a chance. It was hard for me to believe that just a short time ago I never would have thought twice about Mick, and now, he was all I could think about.

As I completed the article and read it back over, I wondered if I would be brave enough to do what I had worked so hard for.

It might mean that Mick would be expelled. It might mean that I would be expelled. I hoped it would end Coach Baker's career, but would it end the entire football team?

I closed my eyes as I considered my options. I could pretend that none of this was happening. Coach Baker could operate for years without anyone ever questioning his methods. Mick could go on to a good college and help his stepdad get his business going again. Everything could just stay the same.

But I wouldn't be the same. I would know what Coach Baker was doing. I would know about kids like Ty, who didn't even have a chance at a college scholarship because he wasn't allowed to play. There would be girls like Hallie, who could be kicked off of the cheerleading squad for being friends with the wrong person, and girls like me who might not even have the opportunity to try out, because they weren't the right shape or look.

I couldn't let that continue to happen.

As long as there was corruption with the head athletics director, there would be corruption in every sport at Oak Brook Academy. I had managed to keep both Ty's and Mick's names out of the article, but I knew that Coach Baker might try to take them down with him. It was a huge risk to upload the article to the school's newspaper and I knew that Mr. Raynaud would have a lot to say to me about it. But it needed to be done.

I logged into the website and uploaded the article to be published in the new copy the next morning. By the time everyone got to their first class the next day, I guessed that there would already be chaos.

I closed my computer and sprawled out on my bed. I imagined Mick stretched out on the bed beside me. His fingertips would coast along my cheek. His warm eyes would gaze into mine.

It's alright, Lala.

I smiled as I imagined his voice.

I'm not going anywhere.

My lips tingled at the thought of his kiss, of his arms pulling me close. He had said that all he ever wanted to do was keep me safe.

I turned my head into my pillow and wished that I had done the same for him. Maybe my attempt at protecting him now would make up for the way I'd used him to begin with. Maybe it wouldn't. Only one thing was certain. I no longer had any control over the situation.

I must have fallen asleep mid-fantasy, because when a knock on my door jolted me awake, my room was dark.

"Not now, Cyndi," I mumbled as I lifted my head from my pillow.

The knock came again. Then the knob on my door began to turn.

My heart raced as I watched it move. "Who's out there?" I climbed out of my bed. Graham had warned me. Did he know about the article already? Was he there to hurt me?

"It's me, Lala." Maby pushed open the door, then put her finger to her lips. "Cyndi is sleeping. I can hear her snoring."

"Maby?" I stared at her. "What are you doing here?" I glanced at the clock. "It's after midnight."

"I know, I've been calling you all night." She frowned as she closed the door behind her. "I had to wait until they did the last room checks before I could sneak out to see you. What is going on? Why aren't you answering my calls?"

"Oh, Maby." I sat down on the edge of my bed. "You've been such a good friend to me. But I'm afraid you might not want to be friends anymore after you find out what I did to Mick."

"Oh, the whole using him for information thing?" She waved her hand through the air.

"Uh, yes, actually." I stared at her. "How did you know?"

"He told me. Mick tells me everything." She pulled my desk chair up to the side of my bed.

"And you're not upset with me?"

"What did he expect? You're a reporter. He was doing something he shouldn't have been doing." She shrugged, then she took my hand. "I'm sorry you were going through all this on your own. I wish you'd felt like you could tell me about it."

"I've really made a mess of everything." I sniffled as tears threatened to flow. "I don't think he's ever going to forgive me."

"Now, now." She hugged me and patted the top of my head. "There you go, not trusting him again. Mick is a good guy, like I told you. You just have to have faith in him."

THIRTY-TWO

Maby's words gave me some comfort, but she hadn't been there when Mick walked away. If I were him, I wasn't sure that I would forgive me.

"Just take a few deep breaths and remember who you are, Lala." She smiled as she looked at me. "Everything is going to be so much brighter in the morning, I promise."

"You can't promise that." I shook my head but managed a small smile.

"I can, because I know it's true." She gave me a light hug. "I'm going to let you go back to sleep. But turn your phone back on, alright? I don't want to have to worry about you."

"I will." As I walked with her to the door, it warmed my heart to know that she cared so much. Being part of this group of friends was like joining a family. I just hoped that she was right about everything. It seemed she did have a knack for being right most of the time. "Thanks again, Maby." I hugged her as she stepped out into the hall.

"Anything for you." She winked at me, then hurried down the hallway.

I stepped back into my dorm room and leaned against the door. There wasn't much chance of my getting back to sleep. I'd already slept several hours and now the countdown had begun.

When would Mr. Raynaud notice the article? When would he show up to lecture me and remove me from the school? He had trusted me with the passwords for the website just like he trusted the other students on the staff. It was his way of building a relationship with the students. But I guessed that he would regret that within a few hours.

I sat down on the sofa and thought about Mick. Was he sleeping? Was he wide awake wondering what would happen when the article came out? Was it even a little bit possible that he was awake and thinking about me? I had just unleashed a set of circumstances that could lead to some very serious consequences. Would I be packing my things and leaving school the next day?

Unable to relax, I began to pace back and forth through the living room. But with each step I took, I worried that the floorboard would squeak and wake up Cyndi. I didn't want to have to give her a long drawn-out explanation of what I was doing up in the middle of the night.

It was almost five. Would Mr. Raynaud be up yet? Would he see a notification on his phone that something had been posted on the website? I couldn't stay in the dorm and just wait. I had to get out.

I peeked out the door and down the hallway in both directions. It was close enough to five that I could get away with telling anyone who caught me that I was out for an early morning run. But again, I preferred to avoid having to speak to anyone if possible.

When I saw that the hallway was clear I left the room and hurried toward the steps. Once I made it out into the courtyard,

I breathed a sigh of relief. No one had caught me, no one had stopped me. For a little while longer at least, I could be invisible. My heart pounded as I wondered for the thousandth time if I'd made a mistake by publishing the article.

"Alana!"

The voice was sharp and full of authority.

My stomach twisted as I turned to face Mr. Raynaud.

I'd thought I would have at least a little more time.

"Mr. Raynaud, I can explain."

"No, you can't." He stopped in front of me and pushed his glasses up on his nose. "You absolutely can not explain. Didn't I deny your request to write an article on this topic?"

"Yes, but—"

"Didn't I make it clear that all articles posted on the newspaper's website must be approved by me first?" He narrowed his eyes.

"Yes, but—"

"No!" He held up one hand as he looked at me. "I believed in you, Alana. I really thought that you could have a future as a journalist, but this has made it clear to me that you can't respect boundaries or rules."

"I had to get the truth out there." I searched his eyes. "Can't you understand that? Isn't that a journalist's first job?"

"You're not a journalist. You're a student." He shook his head. "A student that attends this school, and now I have to figure out how I'm going to explain this to the administration. Alana, I could lose my job over this." He took a sharp breath. "My phone hasn't stopped ringing all morning. Everyone wants answers and I'm playing catch-up, because I have no idea what is going on here. I hope you really have the evidence to back up this accusation because if not—"

"I do." I stared into his eyes. "I do, Mr. Raynaud. It's all true.

I know I might get expelled. I didn't know you might lose your job." I frowned as I looked at the ground. "I'm sorry about that. I knew there would be consequences. But you've always taught me that the most important thing is the truth. I couldn't just stand by and let this keep happening."

"No, I suppose you couldn't." He sighed. "Alana, it's a good article, a very good article." He met my eyes as I looked up at him. "But you're right about those consequences. I'll see what I can do to help you—really, to help us both. But I can't make any promises."

"It's okay." I felt a smile spread across my lips as I sensed that I had his support. "I'm prepared to take whatever punishment the school has to give me, as long as it means that Coach Baker is exposed."

"It certainly looks like he will be. For now, lay low, okay?" He frowned. "Don't stir up an ounce of trouble today. Go to your classes and try not to get caught up in any conversations about the article."

"Okay." I nodded and took a deep breath. "I can do that."

"And I'm going to need to know your sources." He sought my eyes as I looked away from him. "Alana, I need to know who took those pictures and wrote those notes."

"That I can't do." I shook my head. "I can't tell you that."

"Alana, this isn't a game." His voice hardened.

"Mr. Raynaud, giving up a source would be unethical." I pursed my lips.

"You're a student, Alana, not a journalist." He crossed his arms.

"Not today." I looked into his eyes. "Today I wrote an article about a crime that is taking place at a school I am very proud to be part of, and I don't care what the consequences are, because it's more important to me that Oak Brook Academy's reputation remains stellar. Today, I am not a student, I am a journalist. You might not see it that way, but that is the way it is."

"Ugh, to be young and full of ideals again." He pressed his hand against his forehead. "Fine, don't tell me who your source is. But the principal is going to find out and it will look a lot better if you both come forward before he does." He turned and walked away.

THIRTY-THREE

On the way to my first class that morning, I watched for any teachers headed in my direction.

As the hours ticked past, I waited, expecting that at any moment I would be summoned to the principal's office.

Instead, it had been quiet. Even in my first class, most people didn't pay any attention to me. Had Mr. Raynaud taken down the article before anyone could read it? Had all my work been for nothing? It made me sick to my stomach to think that the school might play cover-up. But that wasn't the worst feeling. The worst feeling was knowing that when class was over, when the halls filled with students, Mick wouldn't be out there looking for me.

As I stepped into my second class, I noticed that everyone looked up at me, including the teacher.

"Alana." She locked her eyes to mine. "You need to report to the principal's office."

"Don't I need a pass?" My throat tightened.

"No, just get there quickly." She turned back to the other students and began the lesson for the day.

As I stepped back into the hall, my chest filled with dread.

This was it. This was the moment when my entire life would change.

When I reached the principal's office, I felt the pressure of needing to explain myself. Would he agree that I had done the right thing? Would he cover things up? I wasn't sure what to expect.

"You can go in." The receptionist nodded to the wooden door that I'd been staring at.

I reached for the doorknob, then drew my hand back. Maybe I could just walk away. Maybe I didn't have to go through all this. But wouldn't that make me a student and not a journalist? I took a deep breath, then turned the knob.

As soon as the door swung open, I looked straight into Mick's warm, beautiful eyes. He looked back at me, as if he might be as startled to see me as I was to see him.

"You said you would leave her out of this." He frowned as he turned his attention back to the principal.

"Why is he here?" I lingered in the doorway.

"Come inside and sit down." Principal Carter pointed to the chair beside Mick.

As I sank down into it, my mind raced. Had they figured out that Mick was my source? I looked over at him, but he kept his eyes focused on the carpet beneath his shoes.

"Mick came to me today and told me that he was the source for the information you included in your article." Principal Carter looked at me. "Is that true?"

"Why would you do that?" I stared at Mick, despite the fact that he refused to look at me. "No." I looked back at the principal. "No, that's not true."

"Don't lie." Mick snapped out his words and shot me a brief look before he returned his gaze to the carpet. "I told him the truth; it's what I should have done from the beginning."

"Coach Baker didn't give him any choice." I stood up from my chair. "He shouldn't get in trouble for any of this."

"And you?" The principal sat back in his chair. "Do you think you should get in trouble for any of this?"

The question caught me off guard. How was I supposed to answer? Did he want me to tell him that I thought I should be kicked out of school?

"I'd be more concerned about what you're going to do about Coach Baker." My muscles tensed as I realized that my tone was less than respectful. Was I digging a deeper hole?

"Coach Baker has been removed from this school and the entire football team is going through an evaluation to ensure that the players who are on the team deserve to be on the team. There will also be an open try-out for the cheerleading squad next week." He tilted his head to the side as he looked at me. "I'm glad that this matter was brought to my attention. I certainly wouldn't want anything like this happening here. I'm sorry that several of my students felt they couldn't come to me with this problem. Including you." He shook his head. "That's what concerns me the most. Not that you wrote the article or that you broke the rules, but that you didn't see coming to me first as an option. Why is that?"

"I just thought you might not believe me." I frowned as I looked at him.

"You were wrong." He gestured to the chair behind me. "Please, sit down."

I sat back down. In the process, I brushed my hand against the outside of Mick's. The physical connection sent a shock through my system. When I looked over at him, I found him looking at me. I turned back to the principal.

"I'm sorry that I didn't take the right steps. But Mick shouldn't be punished for any of this. If it weren't for him, I never would have gotten to the truth. He was brave enough to come forward and—"

"You don't have to sing his praises to me, Alana. I'm just sorry that he suffered this long. Mick, you can go back to class." He nodded to Mick.

Mick stood up and stepped past me. I felt his closeness as his leg brushed against my knee on his way to the door.

"Alana didn't do anything wrong either." He paused at the door. "She was the brave one. It took a lot for her to go through with publishing that article."

"That may be, but in the process, she did break a few rules. Thanks, Mick." He nodded to Mick again, then pointed to the door.

Mick stared at me for a long moment, then stepped out.

I braced myself for the next words the principal would speak. I would be expelled. But all I could think about was the way that Mick had looked at me. Was there a spark of warmth in his eyes? Was there a hint of desire still?

As the principal lectured me on proper steps to take and the importance of the rules that were in place, I nodded when I was supposed to, I apologized when it seemed like I should, but my heartbeat quickened at the thought of Mick's eyes on me.

Maybe he didn't hate me after all. He had turned himself in as an attempt to protect me. That had to mean something, didn't it?

"Alana, are you listening to me?"

"I've very sorry." I frowned.

"You're very sorry that you can stay?" He raised an eyebrow.

"What? Oh, I meant, thank you. Thank you very much. I appreciate your letting me stay and I promise I will do my best to uphold the rules of Oak Brook Academy in the future."

"Listen, Alana. I have to give you a hard time over the rules that you broke, but I want to make it clear to you that what you did here was commendable. I just hope that the next time you run into a problem like this, you'll feel comfortable coming to me first." He looked across his desk at me. "Will you?"

"Yes, sir." I smiled at him. A wave of relief washed over me. I wouldn't have to pack up, I wouldn't have to leave. Which meant there might still be time to make things right with Mick.

THIRTY-FOUR

After the meeting with the principal, I headed straight for the bathroom. I needed a few minutes to compose myself before I went back to class. I was relieved that Mick wasn't in trouble and that I wasn't either. But the tension of the day was still thick.

As I splashed some water on my face, I thought about the way that Mick had looked at me. It wasn't anger that I'd seen in his eyes. It wasn't hatred. But that didn't necessarily mean that he was ready to forgive me. With all these thoughts flowing through my mind, I leaned back against the sink and closed my eyes.

When the bathroom door swung open, I straightened up, determined to look calm and together for whoever it was.

"There you are." Maby crossed her arms as she smiled at me. "Aren't you just a troublemaker?"

"I guess I am." I forced a smile.

"Aw, you've had a rough morning, haven't you?" She hugged me, then looked into my eyes. "It's more than just the article, isn't it? What's going on?"

"It's Mick." I showed her my phone. I'd sent a few texts

since the meeting, but he hadn't responded to any of them. "He won't talk to me." I frowned. "Not that I blame him. But if he won't even speak to me, then how can I ever hope to change anything?"

"I understand what you're saying, I just don't know what I can do to help." She shook her head. "I tried to talk to him, but he just shut me down. He seems pretty upset."

"I know." I closed my eyes. "It's my fault. I know it is."

"No one has to be at fault here. The important thing isn't who is to blame, but who is brave enough to get over it." She patted my shoulder. "He's a good guy, remember?"

"He is, he really is." I sighed as I looked at her. "I wish that I had listened to you from the beginning. You told me that he was a good guy, but all I saw was a jock who couldn't possibly be interested in me. Even after he let me into your world, even after he made it clear that he was interested. Honestly, I could have handled being kicked out of school, but I'm not sure that I'll ever be okay with the idea of Mick's never speaking to me again."

"Neither of those things is going to happen." Maby smiled as she walked toward the bathroom door. "Don't worry. I can handle this."

"What do you mean?" I watched as she pulled out her phone.

"Don't worry about it. Just be at the hideout at lunchtime. Can you do that?"

"Yes, I can." My heart pounded. "Do you think he'll show up?"

"Just be there." Maby winked at me as she stepped out the door.

I took a deep breath and turned back to the mirror. The girl who stared back at me had changed a lot in a short time. Never would I have imagined getting a coach fired or falling in love with a jock. Never would I have imagined the intensity of the heartbreak I would experience.

If there was any chance of getting Mick back, I had to take it. I wasn't sure what Maby's plan was, but I knew that if anyone could pull off a miracle, it would be her.

During my last class before lunch, I waited on the edge of my chair for the bell to ring. Technically students could only be in the cafeteria, the courtyard, and the library during lunch. Which meant that only hours after I'd promised Principal Carter that I'd uphold the rules of Oak Brook Academy, I was going to break them.

When the bell rang, I didn't hesitate to jump up. I couldn't get to the hideout fast enough. Would he be there?

When I arrived, I found the building empty. There was still time. He could still show up. I paced back and forth inside the building for a few minutes. Then I decided to get a better view.

I headed up onto the roof so that I could see him if he approached. When I spotted him heading toward the building, I ducked down. If he saw me, he might change his mind about meeting me.

After a few minutes, I heard him on the steps that led to the roof.

My heart pounded. *Please, Mick, just give me a chance.* I watched the door as it began to swing open.

"Maby?" He poked his head through the door. His gaze swept across the expanse until it settled on me.

"Mick, please don't leave." I walked toward the door.

"What is this, some kind of trick?" He stepped all the way out onto the roof and closed the door behind him. "Maby asked me to meet her here, not you."

"Maby told me to be here at a certain time." I frowned. "I didn't know exactly what she had in mind. But I did want to talk to you."

"I noticed." He shoved his hands into his pockets and looked out at the sky. "Lots of voicemails."

"I'm sorry." I paused in front of him. "Mick?"

"I don't know what you want me to say." He kept his head turned away from me.

"I just want a chance to explain things." I traced my fingertips along the back of his hand, hoping that he would let me take it.

His fingers stretched out slightly as if his instincts were to hold my hand, but he balled them up instead.

"I don't want to hurt you," he whispered. "But I don't think there's anything that you can say that will explain what happened between us."

"It was completely unexpected." I tried to meet his eyes. "Mick, I had no idea that I would feel the way I do about you."

"No, you just thought you could get some information out of me." He finally looked at me, his lips tight and his eyes narrowed.

"Because I wanted to be a cheerleader. Okay?" I rolled my eyes as I sighed. "This all started because I wanted to be a cheerleader and because I didn't look the part. I didn't even get a chance."

"Really?" He met my eyes.

"Yes. When I started to look into the way the cheerleading squad was run, I noticed that Coach Baker had a lot of say over that too. Then I began looking deeper into the football team. Once I started discovering evidence, I couldn't look back. I became determined to make it fair for everyone who wanted to be part of the team. So yes, I was focused on that. And no." I frowned as I looked back into his eyes. "It never crossed my mind that you could really be interested in me. The first few times we spent time together, I thought you were planning a prank to get back at me for forcing my way onto the cheer-leading squad."

"And then I pushed you in the pool." His eyes widened. "I didn't realize."

"I know you didn't—well, now I know that. But then, I didn't know what to think."

"What do you think now?" He stared at me, his warm eyes as beautiful as ever. "I'm not just some dumb jock anymore?"

THIRTY-FIVE

"I never thought you were a dumb jock, Mick."

"Don't lie." He smiled a little as he pushed his hair back from his eyes.

"I'm not lying." I caught his hand and held onto it. "Mick, please, just consider forgiving me. Maybe you can't look at me the same way anymore. Maybe you think I'm a terrible person, but I—"

"I could never think that." His hand tightened around mine as he looked into my eyes. "Never."

My words caught in my throat as I was swept away by the warmth in his eyes. Should I kiss him? Should I just lean in and—

"You're not a terrible person." He released my hand and turned away from me. "Things just got a little crazy."

"They don't have to be crazy. I'm sorry. I'll say it millions of times if it will make a difference." I winced as I saw his shoulders tense.

"Stop." He turned back to face me as he shook his head. "Stop apologizing. Alright? Apologizing isn't going to make anything better."

"Then let me make it up to you. Tell me how I can." I searched his eyes. "Mick, I'll do anything."

"Just stop." He took a step back and frowned. "I'm sorry, okay?"

"You have nothing to be sorry for." I caressed the curve of his cheek. "Mick, you didn't do anything wrong."

"Yes, I did." He caught my hand and pressed it against his cheek for a moment, before he pushed it away. "The problem isn't that you thought I was a dumb jock, it's that you were right. You were right to suspect me. I was involved in something terrible. You sensed that about me. You knew that I was no good, and I guess in a way, I did con you. That's what I've been trying to figure out. I got so angry at you. I got so upset that you would treat me that way. But the truth was, I was lying to you the whole time and you just saw me for who I really am." He shoved his hands into his pockets as he took a step back. "Like the principal said, if I'd just come forward right away, maybe I could have stopped all of this from happening."

"Mick, you didn't have a choice, I know that." I tried to meet his eyes. "It's not your fault that Coach Baker took advantage of you."

"It's my fault that I wasn't brave enough to do something about it." He frowned as he looked at me. "At least not until I met you. But the truth is, I'm not good enough for you. You deserve to be with someone who doesn't lie, who can't be manipulated into doing something terrible. That's why this can never work, Alana." He turned back toward the door. "So please, just stop."

"Mick! That's not true! I want to be with you. There's no one else I want to be with." I reached for him, but he was already through the door.

"I have to go." He pulled the door closed.

I heard him run down the steps. As I looked out over the edge of the building, I saw him jog toward the cafeteria.

I wanted to chase after him, but what difference would it make? He wouldn't listen. He wouldn't believe me. I had to find a way to get through to him that he couldn't ignore or walk away from. I had to show him just how much I cared. But I wasn't going to be able to do it alone.

Despite the chaos of the morning, the afternoon football and cheerleading practices were still on. I knew that I would have a chance to see him then. Maybe he would refuse to talk to me, but that didn't mean that I wouldn't be heard.

When I arrived at practice, I found Sherry missing and Hallie in uniform.

"What's going on?" I smiled at her as I joined her and the other cheerleaders.

"Thanks to your article, I'm back on the team." She smiled even wider. "And I'm the new captain."

"That's wonderful news! I can't think of a better person for the job."

"Thanks." She shrugged. "Sherry is going to be in a bit of trouble for a while and she was removed from the squad. It's going to take a little time to get things back on track, but I think we can all work together."

"Great, because I need a favor."

As the football team took the field, I noticed that Ty and Mick led the pack. There was no sign of Graham or Coach Baker. Mick appeared to be running the practice.

As soon as they started running some plays, the cheerleading squad began our routine. As we went through the movements and the chant, I noticed that the football players stopped to watch.

This was it. This was my chance to make sure that Mick heard what I had to say.

As I flipped through the air, I gathered my strength from being in motion and landed firmly on my feet. Then I raced up the empty bleachers. The rest of the cheerleaders followed after me, creating a triangle that led to the very top of the bleachers where I stood.

"Mick!" I shook my pom-poms to get his attention. "This cheer is for you!"

Mick stared up at me, his eyes wide and his mouth half-open.

I felt foolish, but I didn't care. I had his attention.

"You fought and you won! You made things better for everyone! Now it's my turn to fight, and I will—with all my might!" I shook my pom-poms again.

I heard some laughter and a few cheers, but I didn't care. I was focused on Mick, who continued to stare at me.

"You can run, you can try to hide, but it won't change how I feel inside! I love you, Mick. I'll say it a million times. I love you, Mick, and I'll do anything to make you mine!" I shook my pom-poms again, then tossed them aside.

As I launched myself through the air, I tried to focus on the bleacher I needed to land on, but all I could think about was Mick.

Had I made things worse? Had he actually listened to the words I'd shouted?

THIRTY-SIX

My heart pounded as I wondered if I'd made a huge mistake. What if he hated the spectacle that I'd made? What if he wanted nothing to do with me after this? I guessed that wouldn't be much different than where we were before the mortifying cheer. It was too late to change things now.

I landed on the bleacher with a jolt to my ankles. As I straightened up, I glanced in the direction of the field. The other football players were there, many of them laughing.

But Mick was gone.

The rest of the football team was either cheering or laughing. A few of the boys, including Ty, were chanting Mick's name. One of them had gotten their own set of pom-poms and he was running around waving them above his head as he shouted for Mick.

I'd embarrassed him. He'd run off to get away from me. Why did I ever think that this was a good idea?

Embarrassed, I started to head down the bleachers, but my foot slipped at the edge of one of them. I rocked forward, then overcompensated by leaning back. And the next thing I knew, the sky was above me and I was falling. *Way to make it even worse, Alana. Some gymnast. You can't even walk down the bleachers.*

I closed my eyes and braced myself for the pain I would feel when I hit the ground. Instead, I collided with a solid, warm chest. Strong arms wrapped around me. Soft lips trailed across the curve of my cheek and nestled into my hair beside my ear.

"You keep falling for me."

"I do." I laughed as I wrapped my arms around his neck. "I thought you left."

"I didn't." He tightened his grasp on me, then tilted his head so that he could meet my eyes. "I wanted to be right here, right where I was the first time you fell for me." He grinned. "But I didn't think you'd do it again."

"I have a feeling I'll be doing it a lot." I stroked his cheek as I looked into his eyes. "Can you forgive me Mick? Can we give this another try?"

"There's nothing to forgive." He set me down, then pulled me close to him. "You saw me for who I was, even at my worst, and you still loved me. I love you too, Lala. I love your bravery and your strength. I love that you just made a fool out of yourself for me."

"I did, didn't I?" I laughed, breathless, as his words sunk in. He loved me?

"It was beautiful. Anything you do is beautiful." He brushed my hair back from my face and sighed as he looked at me. "I promise I will try to be the kind of person you deserve to be with."

"You already are Mick." I touched his cheeks and gazed into his eyes. "You are an amazing person. You've been through so much, and still, you're willing to risk everything for what is right. I couldn't be prouder of who you are. I just hope that you can trust me. I promise, I will give you every reason to trust me from now on."

"I do trust you." He stared into my eyes. "I trust you because you know my heart and I know yours. Lala, can we make this official?"

"Official?" I smiled.

"Will you be my girlfriend?" He tightened his arms around me. "I promise to always catch you. I promise to be the best person I can be for you. I promise not to laugh at your cheers."

"That last one seems like a lie." I grinned at him.

"It's not." He smiled. "So?"

"So what?" I blinked.

"I asked you a question." He laughed.

"Oh!" I gasped, then nodded. "Yes, of course, absolutely. I want to make it official!" I pulled him close. "Does that mean I can finally kiss you?"

"Not if I kiss you first." He sank his hand through my hair as he tilted me back in his arms and kissed me.

The sensation of his lips against mine stirred a flood of tingles through my entire body. I'd been dreaming about another kiss, since the first, but somehow this felt entirely different. It wasn't a hesitant, questioning kiss. It was a kiss filled with certainty, that whatever the future held, we would be in it together. As I wrapped my arms around his waist and deepened the kiss, I felt a sense of connection that I'd never experienced before.

As I broke the kiss to take a breath, he stared into my eyes.

"Lala, I'm so glad that we found one another." He smiled as he studied me.

"Me too." I looked back at him, but only for a moment, before I locked my lips to his again. Now that I could kiss him, I intended to kiss him as often as possible.

He didn't seem to mind as he smiled through the kiss, then pulled me even closer.

Lost in the kiss and the joy that it inspired within me, I

didn't notice anything strange around us, until I heard the cheers. I gasped and pulled away from Mick just in time to see the entire football team lined up with the cheerleaders' pom-poms. As they cheered, the cheerleaders flipped and leaped in front of them.

"Oh, great, I'm never living this down, am I?" Mick laughed as he hugged me.

"We love you Mick!" one of the football players shrieked, then tossed his pom-poms into the air.

I burst out laughing, then threw my arms around Mick's neck. "Sorry, boys, he's mine!" I kissed him again.

It didn't matter who was watching or how embarrassing it might have been. All that mattered was that Mick loved me and I loved him. We'd found each other despite the problems that were stacked against us and I had no intention of ever letting him go.

EPILOGUE

The hallway was packed with students. Some I knew, some were just a little familiar, but all seemed to be in a hurry. My mind was overrun with to-do lists as I tried to make sure that I wouldn't forget anything. Plus, I had an article to edit and publish by the morning. Despite the traffic jam in my brain, one thought surfaced through the rest.

Mick.

Strong arms wrapped around my waist from behind me. Mick pulled me back against him and nuzzled his lips against the curve of my neck.

"I've been looking for you everywhere."

"I'm sorry." I laughed as I turned in his arms to face him. "I've been running around like crazy getting ready for the cheer-leading try-outs."

"I'm so glad you're in charge of them." He brushed my hair back over my shoulders. "I'm sure it will be great."

"I think so." I smiled. "And how is the team shaping up, Captain?"

"Captain." He laughed. "I still can't get used to that."

"You deserve it." I stroked his cheek. "You should be proud of yourself."

"I'm just glad the new coach seems to be a good guy. He's already assured me that every player on the team is going to get field time. With Ty as the quarterback, I think we have a great chance of having a winning team." He shrugged.

"With you on it, there's no doubt." I grinned.

"Ah yes, my greatest fan. You know, I found a pom-pom in my locker already." He rolled his eyes.

"Sorry." I cringed and smiled at the same time. "If it helps any, I meant every word of that cheer."

"Oh, I think the only thing that would help is hearing it again." He raised his eyebrows.

"Seriously?" My eyes widened.

"Seriously." He nodded. "I'm going to need to hear it again. Many, many times."

"I'm not so sure that's a good idea." I laughed as I pulled away from him.

"Oh, I am. I think I need to hear it now." He tugged me back into his arms.

"Right here?" I glanced around the crowded hallway and then looked back at him.

"Yes, right here. I mean, at least you can't fall off the bleachers." He grinned.

"Mick!" I gave him a playful shove. "No way!"

"No way?" He pouted.

"Stop!" I rolled my eyes.

"I'm just kidding." He laughed as he kissed my cheek. "So, are you running off or do you have a few minutes to sneak away with me?"

"Maybe." I smiled as I glanced at the clock on the wall. "I always have time for you."

"Good, because I think the hideout will be empty. We'll have to run, though." He grabbed my hand and pulled me through the hallway.

As I rushed after him, Maby waved to us and laughed as she shook her head. "Slow down, love birds!"

"Never!" Mick shouted back and ran even faster.

When we reached the hideout, he flung open the door and pulled me inside. As he fell down on the cushion in the middle of the floor, he tugged me down on top of him. I met his lips for a kiss.

"Uh, excuse me?" Apple stared at us both, a paintbrush in hand, as she stood at the edge of the cushions.

"Oops." I laughed as I rolled off Mick. "Sorry, Apple, I didn't know you were here."

"Me either." Mick jumped to his feet. "I guess we were a little distracted."

"Seems that way." Apple rolled her eyes and turned back to the image painted on the wall.

"Who is that?" I studied the outline of a face, framed by masses of blond hair.

"No one." She slashed some blue paint over the golden locks. "I'm done here. You guys can have some time alone." She started to brush past me.

"Apple, is everything okay?" I caught her hand and looked into her eyes.

"Great." She smiled at me, then pulled away. "Enjoy." She waved to us, then hurried out the door.

"I think we scared her off." Mick gazed after her.

"On the upside, we're alone now." I turned back to face him.

"Yes, yes, we are." He laughed as he pulled me back into his arms.

His lips met mine for a passionate kiss and the world

swirled around me. It had been an amazing few months since I'd learned to open my heart.

Coincidently, it had been Apple who'd encouraged me in that regard. In the midst of my happiness, I thought about the face that Apple had painted and I had to wonder—had she taken her own advice?

ALSO BY JILLIAN ADAMS

Amazon.com/author/jillianadams

OAK BROOK ACADEMY SERIES

The New Girl (Sophie and Wes)

Falling for Him (Alana and Mick)

No More Hiding (Apple and Ty)

Worth the Wait (Maby and Oliver)

A Fresh Start (Jennifer and Gabriel)

Made in the
USA
Middletown, DE